The Year The Summer Died

The Year The Summer Died

Patricia Lee Gauch

G. P. Putnam's Sons
New York

Library of Congress Cataloging-in-Publication Data
Gauch, Patricia Lee.
The year the summer died.
Summary: Fourteen-year-old Erin feels left behind
when her best friend's attention turns to a boyfriend
and a horse, so she tries to ride in order to win her
friend back.
[1. Friendship—Fiction.   2. Horses—Fiction]
I. Title   PZ7.G2315Ye   1985   [Fic]   85-19244
ISBN 0-399-21114-4

For the invincible captain,
Mel Lee

One

No one expected me on the seven o'clock bus.

So, I admit I wasn't looking for anybody to meet me. In fact the first thing I saw when I came in on the Greyhound that summer was the dummy of a woman with no head standing in the top window of the General Store. Her lacy gown, all old and dusty, went right to the floor, and her bustle stuck out in back of her as if it were trying to tip her out the window. No head and all. Someone must have stuck her there when dresses like that were in style a hundred years ago and forgot her.

But the whole town was like that, sort of forgotten. Just four old Victorian stores—orange, red, gray, blue—all faded and peeling, one of them Mr. Brush's Market where he still lifted cereal off high shelves with a hook on a pole. Nothing in Littleton, Michigan, ever changed, but, you have to understand, I wanted it that way. Just like I wanted the cottage and my old brass bed and the lake and freighters, the Kellys, my crazy grandma and grandpa. . . in fact all of summer, to stay the same. Even the crickets and mosquitos.

Most of all I wanted Laurie and me to stay the same.

"If you'd sit down," the driver muttered, but I was too stubborn to back up into the sweaty seat where I could only see out side windows, because I was too close to getting there. When my sister Kate and I get into one of our famous fights and I won't talk, my math professor father always teases me, "Shy and stubborn is a powerful combination, Erin!" The truth is I may be shy, but I'm not stubborn unless I have something to be stubborn about, and the cottage is something to be stubborn about.

I can't even remember my first summer there except in an old torn photo of me when I was about three, all pudgy and laughing, throwing a stone into the lake, but ever since I can remember, I loved leaving the boring old Connecticut suburb where I lived and coming to the cottage. It was the best part of my year.

I didn't even wait for the bus to back into the post office lot that day to let us off before I started pulling my suitcase off the rack, nearly dropping it on a huge woman who sat like a brown toad in an aisle seat. I didn't mean to be impolite, but I was in a hurry.

"You need help with that thing?" the driver said, wiping tobacco juice out of the corner of his mouth as he stopped the bus.

Without even answering him, I hiked up the brown case, which had been my sister Kate's before she got a fancy new gray one for graduation, and, hugging it, climbed out of the bus and started down Main Street toward the highway. I had decided to surprise my grandparents before the bus even stopped.

Night comes on late in a Michigan August and, as I dragged my suitcase down the shoulder of the road, it was still light. Trucks went rattling by me—one with crates of chickens and feathers blowing through the cage bars and smelling like a farmyard. A blond boy hung out of a car window to flirt as I passed the snowmobile shop that doubled as a hardware store but I didn't pay any attention.

I did stop at old man Papoletti's fruit stand where I bought a box of raspberries. But only for a minute. He squinted these dark old, wrinkled eyes and, with me standing right there in front of him, asked, "You back?" I nodded, admitting I was, quick squeezed the bag of raspberries into my pocket and started on. I was just "summer people" to him.

I didn't really slow up until I got out on the highway. See, out there away from the village I could be Montana.

Not the state, the person. *Montana Smith.* That was me. I must have been around ten when Laurie and I first played Montana and Denver because that was the year I sort of woke up in the world and wrote in some water left on the kitchen counter: I have begun to understand *this year!!!* signed Erin Cavanaugh, 10 years old.

Of course my mother wiped the water off the counter, and I know now that I knew a lot more at eleven and twelve than I did at ten, and if I had to pick a year when I really began to understand, it would have to be the year I turned fourteen, the year the summer died.

But I am getting ahead. The year I was ten was the first summer I went to the cottage without my sister (Queen Kate, I called her) and the summer Laurie Kelly and I really got to be friends.

I guess I always loved everything about Laurie Kelly, even though she was almost three years older than me. The way she laughed in a low whisper, the way she teased me all straight-faced ("Erin, you'd believe an elephant flew gold to the moon," she'd say.), even the way she looked, always wearing that white ten-gallon hat with her long curly black hair and these soft blue eyes. And we always did a lot together, slept, ate, swam. But that summer we began horse-watching together and that's what started it all.

See, there's not a farm around Littleton that doesn't have an old horse or pony stuck out in a pasture that some farm kid used to ride but didn't anymore, and Laurie and I would hang over fences together wishing we could ride one of those horses, like you hang in front of the General Store wishing someone would buy you a chocolate cone.

Then, one day we were nosing around in my grandpa's workshop, and we found these old boat ropes, sand still in them, and we turned into Montana and Denver on the spot. Grabbing the ropes like lariats or something, we ran down the stairs to the beach and galloped along the shore, our hair waving out, slapping our make-believe ponies on their rumps, and hollering. ·

Where you going, the tall girl said. Nowhere particular, Montana said. Then join up with me, Denver's the name. What's in it for me, Montana said. A fine white pony with a mane to her knees, a far cry from that old calico yer ridin. That all? Montana said. A valley of ponies that'll bring a pretty price. So Montana nodded and jist that easy the two rode off across a pink desert where rocks stuck up like fingers.

We played Montana and Denver all the time after that, inventing Black Bart and his brothers next. We'd wait until near dark or a Sunday morning when everyone was away somewhere, then we'd sneak down to the beach and run wild and free, Bart and his brothers right on our heels.

As long as Laurie and I were together nothing else mattered.

I couldn't even see the cottage until I turned down the driveway. Small and red with a big stone fireplace, it was once a farmhouse right on the highway until some farmer moved it to the lake. Now it's buried back in these huge pine trees on a bluff, its gray roof pulled low over the sides like a shepherd's hat or something. But seeing it, I got so excited I started to run, dragging the suitcase behind me.

When I got to the back door, though, it was locked, and when I looked through the old wavy glass windows, I looked right through an empty house to the lake. Without even stopping, I crawled in the bathroom window of the cottage and called all over the house, but no one was there. I tried the Kellys' by phone, but no one answered, and when I went upstairs and stood up on my bed to shout across to the Kellys' cottage, right over the trees like Laurie and I did sometimes, all of their windows were dark.

I started running from room to room to see if there were any clues where my grandparents were. Taking the stairs by twos, I ran down and searched the papers and rockers on the porch, I ran out back and checked Grandpa's tool shed where he hides when he wants to get away from "civilization." Then, really out of breath, I doubled back and checked the dining room. Everything was there, just the way I remembered it, the Blue Willow plates, the lion-toed table, even the blue braid rug where my grandfather's dog had had an accident and Grandma's Clorox had turned the spot white. But there was no clue about my grandparents.

Some surprise, I thought. Then, all of a sudden, I realized it was nearly dark, and I *didn't recognize all the shadows.* I threw the dining room doors open and ran out on the porch as if I were getting away from something—I don't know what. I was just happy to see the freighters steaming by out on the lake, their lights flickering like streetlights or something, when I heard voices out back.

The back door opened, and my grandmother backed

into the room all plump and dressed in army fatigues and a navy blue sweatshirt and carrying a basket of plants. I ran into her arms like a two-year-old who had gotten lost in a department store.

"Grandma!" I squealed.

"Erin!" She looked surprised all right, then she started to laugh and hug me, "Where did you come from, Pumpkin?" And my grandfather came up behind us, grinning, his captain's hat flattened on his head and his cigar, half smoked and smelly, tight between his teeth.

"At least you saved me a trip to town," he grumped, but he had that glint in his eye.

"Grandpa," I shouted, "you old crab!" and I let go of my grandma and hugged him.

"Watch out, you'll mess my hair," he muttered, and I took off his cap and, pulling his head down, kissed the top of his bald head, even though there wasn't a hair on it.

I was so glad to be back. I sank into the wicker rocker feeling as if I could explode I was so happy—finally summer was starting—when I heard this buzz. I saw my grandfather's face grow dark, and he walked slowly toward the door.

"It's him again," my grandmother whispered.

"Who?" Squinting, I tried to see out of the screen. Moonlight sort of spilled through the trees lighting the edge of the bluff that curved toward the lake like the apron of a dark stage or something.

The buzz—whatever it was—was louder now and hollow and roaring toward our waterfront.

"*What is it?*" I whispered again, not certain why we were whispering, but all at once my grandfather grabbed a flashlight from under the wicker table and ran out to the wooden stairs that led down to the beach, bouncing the beam of light in front of him.

My grandmother quickly tucked her sweater tighter around her, and pulled me outside to the edge of the dark bluff.

I didn't know what to think. The noise seemed to be roaring past the Mullins' beach next door and I could see my grandpa, midway down the stairs, jiggling the beam of light as if he were searching for the noise. But the light just swept across the dark lake and got nothing.

"Thomas!" my grandmother called out. "Come up here! *Thomas!*"

Then suddenly, right in front of our cottage, the spot of light caught a shadowy motorcyclist crouched over his bike, speeding across the hard sand nearest the water, almost touching the waves with its wheels. Something glinted on the back of the guy's jacket as he rode across my grandpa's light, and Grandpa charged down the last steps.

"That's my beach!" Grandpa yelled out at him, his flashlight beam sweeping after the cyclist.

"Screw you!" the motorcyclist shouted back and escaped the light. In another few seconds it was as if the noise had been suddenly stuffed into a huge can and muffled, and the rider had disappeared past the rock jetty down the beach.

Grandpa was panting when he came stomping up the stairs, gripping the rail that ran along them. His cap had fallen off somewhere.

"I'll get him," he muttered. "I swear I'll get him!"

"There's no use of it, Thomas," Grandmother scolded after him. "What if he came after you, a seventy-year-old man." I could tell she was really worried.

But Grandpa pushed right by both of us, still grumbling to himself, and on the porch, he flicked off the flashlight and threw it in a pile of papers scattered under the wicker table.

11

"We'll just see," he said, then, turning, he went inside and climbed the crooked stairs that led up to their attic bedroom.

My grandma put her arm around my shoulder, she had dirt on the tip of her nose. "Was your bus trip all right, your mom said you'd be on the ten o'clock bus, I papered your room, there's lemon cake in the refrigerator," she was saying, but she kept looking up at the ceiling as if she could look through it.

I was sort of settling in on the white rocker for a long talk, I mean, we had a year to catch up on and I was bursting to hear about the summer people, the Kellys' new baby, the Tracys and the Mullins—and Laurie, I could hardly wait to hear about Laurie! But my grandmother's eyes kept looking up at the ceiling, and finally right in the middle of my sentence about how Mr. Papoletti had asked this really silly question at the fruit stand, she patted my hand.

"I'd better go see how Grandpa's doing, dear."

Her wedding ring was lost in the fat on her fingers, but I always liked her warm touch. "You don't mind, do you?" She squeezed my arm and went to the stairs. "There's lemon cake in the refrigerator."

When I heard their bed creak upstairs as if someone had crawled in and was turning over in the covers, I felt as if someone had bumped me in the stomach. See, when you wait practically a whole year, when you scratch off the days on a calendar hanging on your closet door every single night, you don't want everyone to go to bed as if you weren't there. Really you don't.

I just sat out on the porch trying to get something back, even though I wasn't sure then what was lost.

Two

_Mornings when the mist rose out of the valley Montana
didn't stop to wash or start a fire for chow. She snapped
her fingers and out of the whole herd her pony White came
trotting to her, throwing his long white mane and
whinnying. She jumped on and galloped into the mist,
chewing on a piece of rawhide for a little vitamin. Denver
didn't like Montana dragging when she wanted to get an
early start._

I had to see Laurie. Pulling the low pine branches aside,
in the morning before breakfast I ducked under the tree
and jumped the shallow part of the ravine just behind
Grandpa's shed, so excited I could hardly run. _It had been
ten months!_

The four cottages of what we called the summer people
strung along the bluff like nests on a limb or something,
each one separated by a line of birch and pine trees. The
Mullins' cottage next door was the smallest, nothing but a
white frame box with a clothesline of wet bathing suits,
and as I ran I looked to see if there were any signs of John
or his eight-year-old sister Steffie.

John Mullin was a little older than I was and Laurie's twelve-year-old sister Bridie Kelly had a big crush on him, but John Mullin was not my favorite person and his eight-year-old sister drove me crazy trying to follow me around. I was almost glad the shades were still pulled.

The Kellys' was the third cottage, nearly as old as ours, with pine-board smells I could smell even standing on the back porch and linoleum with worn-out yellow flowers on the kitchen floor, probably worn-out from the six Kelly kids fighting on it over who was going to do dishes or something. The minute I started up the back stoop, old Fritzie, the Kellys' swayback dachshund, started barking even though he couldn't see, or maybe because he couldn't see.

Through the screen I could see figures moving around the kitchen.

"Hello, Grandma Kelly, Laurie here?" I could tell by the shape it was old Mrs. Kelly because she was hobbling around on a walker she called Henry and had ever since I could remember.

"You back, Erin?" she asked and I thought of Mr. Papoletti asking the same dumb thing, but the difference was I loved Grandma Kelly.

"I am, Grandma Kelly," I said. "I'm looking for Laurie."

"I've got cookies." She hobbled toward me on Henry. "You're oatmeal, aren't you?"

"I am but I need to find Laurie," I said again more urgently.

"Well, you're going to have trouble with that, dearie," she said and she hobbled down the alley of a kitchen and unscrewed the glass jar filled with cookies. I guess that was the first hint I had that something was different.

"Try Sugar's barn," a voice, sounding gruff like Laurie's

dad, shouted from somewhere in the center of the house. Sugar was Laurie's oldest sister and lived alone in a tiny farmhouse up the road that everyone called "the little farm."

The second Grandma Kelly pressed three cookies out a crack in the doorway I started at a run across the field for the highway.

Crossing the highway always seemed like going into a different world to me anyway. It wasn't just that the summer people were all on the lake side, the farm people on the other. It always seemed kind of creepy over there. Ratt Road ran away from the lake through two rows of old chestnut trees, past a deserted schoolhouse whose windows looked like sleepy eyes because some farmer had nailed boards around part of them, past empty fields and barns that were half broken apart.

Usually what I was afraid of most walking down Ratt were the German shepherds which every farm around Littleton seemed to have, none of them tied up. I used to think they just waited for me, big and snarly-teethed, ready to tear across the yard at my legs and I would practice taming them with my supercool voice.

But that day as I started past Papoletti's orchard, it wasn't just creepy. I realized the orchard with its old twisted apple trees was a perfect hiding spot.

Bart! Suddenly, Montana knew it was an ambush! She could smell him. "Denver," she wanted to shout. But Denver wasn't there, and that ugly rustler might be one fierce outlaw, always smelling of tobacco or beer, and ready to gun his best friend down for a good horse, but he wasn't going to get Montana. She whipped that pony and ran.

My heart was pounding like fists against the inside of my shirt, when I reached the beginning of Sugar Kelly's farm, and I heard this voice from somewhere in the bushes shout,

"Hey!"

I stopped short, scared, you know, my neck all hot and wet, expecting to see Bart and his pistol staring at me through the weeds but all I could see was a ditch full of blue cornflowers waving in the wind that always blew down Ratt Road from the lake.

"Over here." When I stepped off the road, I saw a tuft of brown hair and John Mullin with wire cutters in his hand.

Bare-chested and sweaty, he kind of glistened squatting down by the fence post. But over John's head for the first time I could see Sugar's barn. It was nothing more than a big garage with a rippled aluminum roof but if Laurie was anywhere, that's where she was, so I waved to him and practically stumbled back toward the road I was in such a hurry.

"I see you're still shy," he called after me and laughed, standing up and circling his one arm with his hand. Coming from him, I thought that was interesting because he never did put more than two words together at a time, even though Bridie Kelly thought he was a miracle. But I guess I shouldn't have been surprised that he would say or do something dumb. Last summer he'd sit in the toolshed with my grandfather and they'd play with an air compressor my grandfather had built from some kit. Imagine getting excited over an air compressor? All it did was squirt air!

"No, I'm not shy," I said. In my head I could tame German shepherd dogs with my cool voice, no biscuits needed. I could ride the range for fifty miles without stopping for water. *I could outrun Bart.*

He laughed, and his voice cracked sort of shyly, it seemed to me, and I almost told him, but he turned and started back across the ditch, tucking the wire cutters into his back pocket. "You ought to come with us tonight to the old Olmstead House," he said with his back turned on me. "Us" meant what Laurie and I always called the "younger kids" even though they weren't really much younger than me: they were Laurie's sister Bridie, her fourteen-year-old brother Danny, and Mary Tracy, our neighbor on the other side, who was thirteen.

"You mean that boarded-up house down Ratt?" I asked, a little curious I admit.

"It's not boarded up anymore," he grinned, sort of sheepishly.

When I didn't answer, he squatted down by the fence and said, "Hey, does Bridie Kelly still bother you? She's not so bad, you know." I guessed he remembered last summer's bonfire when Bridie and I ended up throwing sand out of Coke bottles at each other. Supposedly, just teasing, but the truth is Bridie was the one Kelly I could do without and I wasn't even going to pretend I heard him when I realized that he was working on Sugar's fence.

"What are you doing there?" I sort of blurted out.

Then his face grew red which made his eyes very blue. I didn't remember that from other summers. "Oh, just fixing fences, earning a little spending money."

I didn't ask him what for. I nodded and started to walk away.

"See you," I said, and he turned back toward me for a moment and grinned. I decided what Bridie Kelly liked about him was his smile. He'd look not quite at you, then, as if something pleased him deep inside, this smile would appear out of nowhere. As if it had surprised even him.

"Say, where you going?" he asked.

"To see Laurie."

He shrugged. "She may be busy."

17

"That's okay," I said.

"I mean too busy."

I just grinned. "She's expecting me." Other people never did understand the kind of friends Laurie and I were.

"I hope you're right," he said and left running.

"I'm right," I said.

You say you saw something, Montana? Just Black Bart! Montana said. Then move it, girl, Denver said, and their hooves thundered across the valley.

Sugar Kelly was mucking out a stall when I tiptoed into the barn. The oldest of the three Kelly girls, Sugar was at least twenty-three years old, though it was hard to tell for certain because she never changed, except I noticed each year her hands got tougher and tougher like the outside of shoes.

Part of the reason for this was that Sugar Kelly played guitar at a bar out on the highway and her fingers grew tough from holding the metal strings down, but the big reason was that she ran this little farm across the highway from her family's cottage. It had been nothing but a tumbledown little house with a big shed on a few acres, but she had discovered it and coaxed her father into letting her live there with a few horses if she would put up her own fences and a better barn, which she did without asking much from anyone, though it appeared that John Mullin was helping her this summer.

Anyway, she did all this mainly for a horse named Missy, a big red quarterhorse that was ornery and stubborn but that shone pretty good after she hosed her down. In my head, my pony White could take Missy any day in a race.

I came up behind Sugar without her seeing me. She was shoveling wet manure onto this skinny pitchfork in the first stall and letting the bedding sift through. The wet clumps she threw over her shoulder into this cart she had made out of an old baby buggy. A small fat gray pony hung his nose over the stall door, curling his upper lip as he tried to nuzzle Sugar's back when she passed by.

I tiptoed up behind her and when she was bending over grabbed her waist.

Dropping the fork, she turned and squealed, "Erin! You're back!" and she came over and hugged me, her long arms squeezing me. It gave me such a warm feeling.

"Grab a pitchfork," she said, laughing and putting her arms around mine. Her hands, rougher again, sort of scratched my soft cotton shirt. "See the new barn cats?" A scrawny white kitten, hardly more than born, tottered over the straw, trying to rub against Sugar's leg. "And the foal?" Sugar sort of gathered me in and led me to the middle stall where a baby horse, still a furry tan, teetered to the gate on thin stilt legs. New things were sure wobbly.

"My baby," Sugar purred, scratching its big head, and I reached through the slats to stroke its white nose, not at all sure it wouldn't bite because the truth is, it has never been clear to me whether horses bite or not. I mean, I know they aren't German shepherds, but they do have big teeth.

"Is Laurie around?" I asked her.

"You mean you didn't come to see me?" she grinned, her long hair swinging around her shoulders as she moved, but she knew what I had come for all right. When I didn't answer, she took my hand as if I were an eight-year-old or something and started walking me out of the barn, back to the flat, dry meadow where she usually rode Missy. When we reached the fence, I could see a horse running in the field, a full-sized roan, its mane flying out golden red behind it. Some older girl with a white ten-gallon hat was riding her. *Then I saw it was Laurie—on Missy.*

"Well, what do you think of your friend?" Sugar asked me.

I couldn't believe it! I mean, we had wished horses right out of the sky since I could remember, and here Laurie was on a real one. But when I ran up along the trail next to the fence and Laurie didn't stop and I could hear the horse panting and pumping as she cantered him I thought, *Laurie's riding a real horse.* And I wondered if Sugar had given her Missy and if that meant Laurie would be riding and riding out here in the field by herself every day, and I wondered if it meant she'd be cleaning out the horse manure like Sugar did every spare minute, throwing it into wagons made out of baby buggies, her hands growing rougher and rougher like the outside of shoes. *And I wondered about Montana and Denver. Laurie looked so old!*

"Hey, Montana," Laurie laughed as if she could read my mind, and galloped Missy, the folds of her neck foaming with sweat, towards the fence. When Laurie tried to stop Missy, though, she broke away down the straight stretch of the field.

"Hey!" Laurie said, her face all red as she tried to pull Missy back. I almost felt like I didn't know her.

"Use your knees!" Sugar called out to her.

But then Missy just backed up, throwing her head and swinging her shiny butt from side to side.

"You're pulling on her mouth," Sugar said, "Knees!"

Finally the horse stopped and I thought to myself Denver never had those problems, and I thought the reason was that Denver knew her pony like the back of her hand.

But Laurie laughed, catching her breath. "Dumb horse." Then she looked down along the fence at me with that look I remembered as if we were the most special friends in the world. As if no one else knew what we knew. As if no one else understood each other as we did. That look. And I knew nothing had changed.

And she bent over and scruffed my head with her hand. "Hi, Montana," she said, really soft. "When did you get up, silly?"

To tell you the truth I thought I had written her, but I might not have because when I start packing a lot of things slip by me. "Last night," I said. I started walking alongside Laurie and Missy next to the fence, waiting for just the right opportunity to say "Let's talk" and "Let's meet on the beach" and "The ropes are still out in the garage," but she started talking first.

"There is so much to tell you, Erin," she said.

I knew there was.

"I work Missy out every day—mornings, afternoons."

"Yes." I wanted to tell her that Bart had tried to ambush me from the orchard.

"And I've met this boy, Erin." She hung over the side of the saddle toward the fence to tell me that. "He is gorgeous—a number nine, at least. Black curly hair, and black eyes like night." She looked at me, as if she were a little embarrassed or something. There were a lot of people who thought Laurie was shy, too. "He lives down on Ratt Road in that house with the tar-paper sides."

I must have stopped walking alongside the fence without really knowing I was stopping, because she had to turn the horse around. Maybe my face changed, too, I don't know, because Laurie said, "He wants to meet my friend Montana. He thinks Black Bart is off the wall!" And she laughed.

If you stand still in the middle of a field, it all of a sudden gets noisy. And I must have stood there because I could hear crickets or maybe they were locusts. Kate and I always argue over which noise belonged to which, and we always argue over why they made the noise. Anyway, I guess I must have just stood there, because Laurie stopped and said, "Erin?" and then she said it again, and turned Missy toward me, "Erin?" she said. When she did, Sugar called out from the barn.

"Keep that horse moving!"

"I'm nearly done!" Laurie said over her shoulder.

"Well, then walk her down," Sugar said. "You don't want her muscles to get stiff."

With the ends of her reins, Laurie slapped Missy on her rear and tried to keep her walking straight, but I just stood there. Ten months is a long time of waiting.

"Look, Erin, I'll call tonight, okay?" she said over her shoulder with that slight sweet break in her voice that I could hear even when she didn't turn.

"I do want to hear," I said, but I'm not sure she heard me because she suddenly put her heels into Missy's side and cantered into the far ring. ". . . all of it," I said, mostly to myself.

"I'll call," she said again, and she took off toward the back fence. "I promise."

"She's real pretty, isn't she," Sugar suddenly said behind me. At first I didn't even know she meant the horse. "Would you like a horse like that?"

What I wanted to tell her was that I already had one, a white pony I had found in a valley where man had never stepped before, a pony with a white mane down to her knees, but even Sugar would never have understood.

When I scuffed back to the cottage along the washboard gravel road that led through the chestnut trees like an alley, a rattly gray Plymouth raced down beside me, leaving rolls of dust, but I had one thing on my mind: when Laurie got back to her house, she would call, and we'd sit on the phone and talk and talk. She had a lot to tell me.

By eight o'clock, though, the phone just sat there. It rang exactly once for my grandma: Sears, calling to say her package of stockings had been misdelivered to a Mrs. Bell in a gray shingled cottage with a milk jug of geranium flowers by the mailbox.

Sometime around nine Grandpa shouted out from the bluff, "Another one!" There were two things my grandfather watched, the weather and freighters. He could even call out the names of some, like the giant tanker *Cort,* and he had pulled a lawn chair to the edge of the bluff and laid some huge navigator maps across his lap.

"Erin, come here," he shouted, looking through binoculars toward a string of lights moving through the black.

All I ever saw through the binoculars were my own eyelashes, anyway, but I didn't go out on the bluff. I sat on my grandma's lap even though my feet touched the ground and lay my head back on her soft shoulder.

"Well, my goodness," my grandma said and she started scratching my back in long scratches from my neck right down to my waist. "Grandpa and I are so glad you're here, Erin," she said.

Hot and sweaty, White stumbled over rocks in the empty river bed. Easy, girl, Montana whispered low. Denver had been out ahead but there was nary a shadow of her now, and as the night came on black and thick across the desert Montana knew something had happened—she could feel it prickling under her skin.

Three

~~~~~~~~~~~~~~~~~~~~~~~~~

It was only quarter to eight in the morning and I was still in bed when I heard my grandfather shout, "He ran over the pipe again!"

I had been awake, but just lying there when I heard him. I didn't even look for slippers. Barefooted, I ran down the stairs, jumping the last three, in time to see my grandfather panting as he reached the landing at the top of the steps that led up from the beach. His old navy blue Greek captain's hat was flattened on his head and he had a stub of a cigar in his cheek.

I didn't know what to expect from anything or anyone anymore; it was like there was a big crack in summer.

"Right over the pipe," he said again. "Calley Motors, his shirt said. Calley Motors right over the pipe!"

"I hear you, dear." My grandmother put down her planting trowel and, brushing the dirt from her hands onto her pants, ran to meet him at the landing.

"And *he scratched the pumphouse!*" my grandfather said, as if a terrorist had blown up an embassy. "Left three inches of silver paint right across the door."

"Only three inches, dear," my grandma assured him, putting her arm around my shoulder as I ran up. There was already a piece of dirt on the tip of her nose where she had scratched.

"Damn it, Ethel, that's not the point! That kind of kid won't stop until he gets the whole pumphouse!"

"He'd have trouble running over the pumphouse, wouldn't he, dear?" she said.

But now I began to understand. For as long as I could remember, The Pumphouse had stood for The Cottage in my Grandpa's head. I know, it doesn't make sense, but, see, the pumphouse was this tiny red aluminum Sears special at $359 that he had ordered through a catalogue and put together with his "own hands, damn it." He had bought it to cover this little black motor that pumped water up the bluff from a long pipe laid into the lake. See, we needed water like anyone else and the pumphouse made the pump safe.

But there was more to it than that. My grandpa was convinced that if a storm or waves or anything else ever got the pumphouse, it would take the bluff next, and if the bluff ever crumbled, what could go next but the cottage. So, save the pumphouse, save the cottage!

Now he was pacing the bluff, my father would have said, like a madman, which wouldn't have surprised my father, who always said he couldn't figure out how my mother, who is a normal old elementary school teacher "and just a little neurotic," could have a father like that. "He thinks about no one but himself," my father once told my mother when he thought I couldn't hear. But I think my father was wrong. He never saw my grandpa telling me his Fairview stories in bed at night, about how he had been a tough little kid down on Fairview Avenue. He never even saw my grandpa and me racing around on the lawn mower together in circles as if we were in the Indianapolis 500 race.

Anyway, that morning my grandfather paced to the very edge of the bluff and lifted his binoculars up at the sky. "I'm going to bury that pipe, Ethel! And build a fence around the pumphouse and pile rocks inside the fence!"

"He can climb over the fence, dear."

"It'll keep his damned motorcycle away, won't it?"

I knew he was thinking a fence would keep storms away, too.

My grandfather aimed his binoculars down at the ravine where the run-off water from the bluff ran into the lake and left rocks in the wall of the ravine exposed. "Erin, get the wagon, Ethel, get the sledgehammer . . . I'll get that coil of fence I bought to keep the rabbits out of the garden . . ." It was as if I'd never been gone.

"Well, she's not going to build a fence her second day here," my grandma said, wiping her cheek with the back of her hand and just making the dirt smear worse.

My grandfather looked at her, scowling. "I don't know why not. It's her cottage too."

"Let her go with the kids." No one was asking me if I wanted to go with the kids.

"Kids?" His eyebrows started to run together again. "You mean those Kelly kids and the rest of them, why, those twerps aren't worth seeing, running over people's pipes, hanging out around old deserted houses like bums, that's what they're like, bums hanging out." He looked at my grandma for a minute as if he were trying to see if he had impressed her enough.

"You weren't a kid once?" my grandma said. "On Fairview Avenue, you weren't a kid hanging out?"

I knew she had hit a sore spot. "That was the Depression. During the Depression, you weren't sure if you were going to have enough to eat. On Fairview Avenue, you were hanging out because . . . you . . . couldn't . . . find . . . a . . . job!"

"When you were thirteen you had a job?"

"I had a job from the time I was *nine!*"

They were just standing out there on the bluff shouting at each other as if they were the only two people in the whole world. Arguing was nothing new to my grandfather and grandmother, and to tell the truth I think arguments were a little like storms for my grandfather. Just like sometimes I'd catch him out on the porch sitting right through a thunderstorm enjoying it, sometimes I think he liked to argue.

But when my grandma was done she was done, and suddenly she just puckered her mouth tight, refusing to let one more word out, picked up a flat of flowers she had set down at her feet and turned her back on him. When she had reached the porch she said, softly, but as if she were reading a new law in some town square, "Erin's going to the Kellys' if she wants to."

My grandfather scowled at me, but sort of hurt, his hat off at an angle. Sometimes he reminded me a lot of a little boy.

"I'll help, Grandpa, it's okay." I didn't want to go to the Kellys' anyway.

My grandmother had nails in her mouth and had begun to retack the screen where it had pulled away from the porch frame when I had finally finished dressing and was ready to go down to the beach.

"You just being brave, Erin Cavanaugh?" she looked at me suspiciously.

"No." She still looked suspicious. "Really. But Grandma, Grandpa always liked the Kellys, why doesn't he like them this year?"

27

"Oh, there's been a few pranks."

"What kind?"

"Nothing important . . . pranks."

"Grandma!"

"Oh, Conover's mailbox was smeared with mud down on Ratt Road and someone rolled four bales of hay out on the highway and burned them yesterday morning."

"But that sounds like town kids, or farm kids, but not Kellys. No cottage kid would do that."

"Then there's that cyclist running back and forth on the beach day and night. Sometimes I think he torments your grandfather on purpose."

"But that's not a Kelly either."

"Well, you know people here talk."

"What do they say? Do they think the same kids are doing all these things? Do they think it has something to do with the Kellys?"

But she didn't answer. She kept her eyes on the nail she had placed on the frame where the screen was ripped. "Laurie's all right, darlin', if that's what you're asking." She whacked the nail, then looked back at me and announced, sort of smugly. "Anyone that's with you is going to be just fine."

"Grandma!" Really, sometimes she was impossible.

She looked over her shoulder and smiled. "No scolding, Erin, grandmas have rights, and one of them is to believe that their own grandchild is perfect." She grinned gently at me and gave the tack a light tap.

"Wow!" I laughed and, putting my arm around her shoulder, kissed her on the nose.

I guess it was around nine when I walked down the wet part of the beach, watching my footprints disappear almost the minute I lifted my foot, and made my way into the ravine. I didn't really want to go to the Kellys' and I was just glad to be off alone.

Denver! Montana called as she wound her way through the purple pass. Denver! But her voice echoed into an empty cavern and rocks peered down like ugly faces.

I had managed to dig three pretty big rocks out of the side and was practically buried in prickers when all of a sudden two cold hands grabbed my shoulders from behind.

"Hey!" this little voice said. "You're back!"

"Steffie! I jumped a foot!" It's funny how when you want to be with one person, you don't want to see anyone else. Particularly not some obnoxious eight-year-old you haven't seen for a year, and I think I was really mad at her for not being Laurie.

"It smells in here," Steffie announced, looking up the sides of the ravine as if she were in the middle of a Tarzan movie and not liking it.

"It's stagnant water," I told her and went on pulling on this big salt-and-pepper-colored boulder wedged into the bank.

"This isn't fun, Erin," she said.

"It's not your pumphouse that is being attacked!" I don't know why sometimes she could bring out the eight-year-old in me!

"Is yours, Erin? Is your pumphouse being attacked? Is it?"

"Sort of . . . Look, can you see I'm working, Steffie? Look at me, can you see that?"

"I'll play Montana with you," she said, ignoring me. The day she had spied on Laurie and me we were in a terrible shoot-out with Bart. In fact, Denver lay wounded on the beach, and I had had to gallop alone for help when I ran into Steffie hanging on the birch tree watching. She never let me forget it! "I'll be Wichita," she'd coax when she'd catch me alone. Wichita, you like that? Of all the dumb names.

When I didn't answer her she gave me a quick rundown of her year like some computer printout, about some Mrs. Penny who kept her after school for eight days in a row, about her chicken pox and the scars it left because she scratched. When I still didn't talk, she suddenly started pulling her way up the side of the ravine, knocking down the loose sand around me. Then she turned and slid down, almost into the stream at the bottom of the ravine.

"John still loves you," she said, wiping the mud off the backs of her legs. She had started that stuff last summer when John kept hanging around my grandfather's shed.

"Steffie, that is stupid."

"I told him that you hated him." She started picking the mud from under the rock I was working on, so close I could feel her breathing on my hand.

"Maybe you love Danny Kelly?" she teased, then she sprang up and draped her arms around my neck, almost toppling me. "Or do you just love Laurie?"

I was so mad at her. "Steffie," I practically shouted, "that is dumb. Because you like someone, Steffie, because a person is your best friend, doesn't mean you love them. Not like that. The whole world isn't divided into two and two, you know. Not summer anyway. Sometimes I don't think you know anything about the world, you know that?"

A gray butterfly flew into the bramble on the ravine and, fluttering crazily as if searching a way out, discovered an opening between two limbs and simply fluttered out.

"I know where the Ural Mountains are," Steffie said.

I just stared at her. "That's not enough."

I guess it is always weird to see or hear something when people don't know you're there. But suddenly we heard horses' hooves and maybe they surprised us, because without saying a word to each other, we started crawling along the side of the ravine, watching the beach through the thicket.

That's when I saw Laurie and the boy with the black curly hair and gray cut-off shirt racing bareback down the beach on Missy. I never expected to see that. They flew across the shallow waves, but at a spit of land near us they started into the water on the mare, the boy, hanging onto Laurie's waist, touching her, and she, laughing that whispery laugh.

"Take it easy," he sort of threatened, but he was laughing too.

I felt as if I were hiding behind a curtain watching something I shouldn't.

Missy danced and slipped on the rocks on the bottom of the lake. Then she reared back, her tail swishing across the water as Laurie drove her in farther.

"Easy," Laurie cooed at Missy. The boy hung on tighter.

Honest, I don't know what I expected to see.

"Hey, wait a minute!" Now he laughed in this low voice, but Laurie ignored him and the horse danced further into the lake. I watched, my cheek almost buried against the ravine I was pressing so hard, and I knew I hurt somewhere in the middle of me. *Laurie, oh, Laurie.* Then the boy splashed water up at her, sending sprays all over her legs, and she turned around, and he grabbed her face between his two hands and he kissed her—*he kissed her*—and I felt my heart pounding inside my shirt. She just looked at him, then she suddenly leaned forward and, flapping her legs like wings against Missy's sides, pulled the horse around and ran her through the water toward the shore.

"I'm going to get you, girl!" the boy shouted behind her, wrapping his arms tighter around her waist.

Laurie just laughed and flapped her legs again, galloping the two of them down the beach. And they were gone and I just sat there, looking.

"Maybe if you could ride a real horse Laurie would love you again," Steffie said, and when I still just sat there, she said, "I could ride a horse," and she jumped up on a log fallen across the stream and started bouncing on it.

"That's not exactly a horse, Stef," I said.

"Would you ever, Erin?"

"What?"

"Ride!"

"Why not?" It was really hard to think.

"When?"

"I'll tell you one thing, Steffie, to ride a horse you need a horse, don't you think? Wouldn't that make riding easier?" And besides, I have one, I wanted to say. A white pony with a mane down to her knees, I wanted to say. Oh, Denver, I wanted to say.

That night, lying upstairs in my room, I heard kids below the bluff trailing down the beach, laughing and throwing someone in the lake. I recognized Bridie's voice and Danny's. John's, too, and I was pretty sure I heard Mary Tracy. It was the "younger kids."

When they got right below our bluff, Bridie Kelly shouted up, "Hey, Erin, Erin! Want to go swimming?" Her voice echoed.

I lay curled in my blanket, hoping they'd go away.

But Bridie sang out again "Erin!" and I crawled over to

the window just to shut her up. "Big-Eastern girl, you coming out?" she kept up.

"No," I shouted back, hoping my grandfather's television rerun of *The Odd Couple* was on loud enough so he wouldn't hear.

"Ever?" She called and I heard these low garbled laughs like a tape speeded up.

"Sure . . . sometime!" I said. *Why didn't they go away?*

There were garbled sounds again, then she shouted up, "How about the bonfire tomorrow?"

"Yes, yes," I said back and when they didn't answer I said it again. "All right!" And I said to myself, why not. I didn't like Bridie Kelly. My sister would say, "You're jealous of her, Erin, green as grass," but the truth was, other years Bridie Kelly had stuck to Laurie like glue. Even if Laurie were going to stay overnight with me, Mrs. Kelly would say poor little Bridie would have to stay too and once she crawled in my bed and in the middle of the night I felt warm and wet, right along my leg, and I didn't know what it was, but I was afraid what it was. And it was. I really didn't like Bridie Kelly.

But I had been wrong about everything being two and two. Laurie had a boy with black curly hair and eyes like night and she didn't want me. Or Montana. And summer was still summer and I had checked off all the days of every single night for ten months, and, well, if everyone was two and two—the whole summer two and two!—I would be, and not with any runt like Steffie Mullin.

I curled back into my blanket hearing Felix Unger shouting at Oscar Madison on the TV downstairs, thinking maybe John was right, maybe Bridie wasn't so bad and maybe she knew other kids and I'd meet a whole lot of new people. Maybe even a boy, and maybe I'd like him and maybe even write him in the winter.

Denver had disappeared! Like dust after rain! Montana rode the canyon again and again looking for her, the shadows all purple in twilight and White's hooves clattering on the dry-caked riverbed kicking up stones. The question was what had happened to Denver Kelly?

Four

In the morning the wind shifted to the north and the ripples started rolling in crossways, each one a little bigger than the one before, until they were lapping at the bluff in little bites. That didn't stop my grandfather from working on the pumphouse fence. While I was getting dressed, I saw him pulling the wagon back and forth right through the waves with loads of rocks. I was rinsing my hair in the bathroom tub with my head upside down when all of a sudden a bell started ringing down on the beach. Still dripping, I went to the screen door because my grandfather didn't seem to hear it.

"There's a bell!" I yelled over the bluff.

"Yep!" he shouted back without looking up at me and dumped a load of rocks right in front of the pumphouse, ignoring it.

Then, all of a sudden, it stopped. I stood there for a minute. Nothing. So, water draining cold into my shirt, I ran back to the tub and turned on the warm water. The bell started to ring again. Grabbing a towel this time, I ran into the kitchen.

"Grandma!"

Wiping flour off her hands and with flour sprinkled across her bust, my grandmother started to explain before I had really asked. "Grandpa's invention. The bell will go on when someone's using water and the water pressure is dropping in the pump. But if the bell doesn't go off, something's wrong." I turned around and headed for the bathroom, then stopped.

"So every time I wash my hair, the bell will ring."

She nodded. Then it struck me.

"And every time someone flushes the toilet, the bell will ring?"

She nodded.

"And the whole beach will know."

A nod.

"Every time."

A nod.

"Oh, boy," I said and went back to the sink, drying my hair. "This family is really crazy, you know that, Gram, crazy!" I said from inside my towel. I was glad that I had already gone to the bathroom that morning.

"Maybe not so crazy, dear," my grandmother said as she came up behind me and put her fingers in my towel to help me dry my hair. "Patrolman Jim Anders said three more mailboxes were knocked down on Ratt."

"When?"

"Last night."

"But, Grandma, you even said kids are kids. Even in Connecticut kids are kids."

"Do they ride back and forth over gardens in the middle of the night, too, in Connecticut?"

I turned around and looked at her, surprised.

"Grandpa's garden was so churned up last night we couldn't even see the tire marks that did it—just scattered dirt and broken tomatoes and vines all over like a storm had hit."

I picked up my brush and plopped down on the side of the bathtub.

"I don't know anymore," she said. "I really don't."

I was afraid she wouldn't go to the bonfire.

A bonfire had started every summer I could remember. All the kids would run around scrounging up wood and we'd build this great pyramid of branches and scrap lumber and split trunks on the beach. And everyone would come. Mrs. Kelly and the baby, Old Grandma Kelly and her walker Henry, Mary Tracy's three-year-old sister who loved to throw sand at Steffie Mullin, and all the teenagers. Sugar. Then, we'd all huddle together, warmlike, you know, and someone would light this huge crackling bonfire. You could see it for miles in the dark.

I was just sure the bonfire would put summer back together, but everybody had to come.

I followed my grandmother back into the kitchen. "What summer needs is a beginning, Grandma, don't you see?" I said.

"You're probably right, dear," she said, placing banana slices carefully inside a pie shell.

"Because without beginnings, well, nothing can start."

"I can't argue with that, dear."

I sat down at the kitchen table and looked up at her. "So you'll go to the bonfire?"

"Oh, that's what this is all about." She touched my cheek. "Of course I'll come. I love marshmallows." She didn't seem to connect what happened in the night with the bonfire at all.

But when I asked my grandfather later, he was already gathering his navigator maps out on the bluff and he said,

"Not me!" Until my grandmother nudged him in the ribs. "Well," he said, "I'll go but I won't like it."

Steffie wasn't much better.

"You going to the bonfire?" I asked her through the bathroom screen door later as I blow-dried my hair for the second time that day. She was rubbing her face all the way down the screen, looking as if she had a piece of Play-Doh for a nose.

"I don't think I'm supposed to," she sort of sang.

"Sometimes you are really silly, Steffie, everyone is supposed to go to a bonfire." See, that was the thing about a bonfire. Everyone was supposed to go.

Five

That night as the sky grew darker, the moon came up this buttery yellow ball peeping over the edge of the black lake. Then, as if it were filled with helium or something, it rose slow, a giant yellow thing, melting across the lake water, sort of catching ripples in its buttery light. I loved the lake and the night. I felt terrific.

My grandfather liked to watch the freighters at night if he had a decent moon, but I coaxed him to put his binoculars down, and he and my grandmother trailed across the lawn after me, both hauling these lightweight chairs and a blanket.

"I hate bonfires," my grandfather muttered under his breath when we got to the beach.

"That's silly, dear," my grandmother answered. "No one hates bonfires."

"And I smell rain."

"Thomas," she said, taking his elbow as we started across the sand. "You old fool, there's not a cloud in the sky."

"I don't have to see a cloud to smell a storm," he

39

mumbled as the three of us ducked under the willow branches that separated our beach from the Mullins'.

My heart kept pounding, I admit it. Finally summer was going to begin.

But they had started the fire without us, and, as soon as I caught sight of the flames spitting up into the night from the giant pile of wood, I knew something was wrong. It was the shapes. There were no Grandma Kelly shapes, no baby shapes, no Mrs. Kelly nursing shapes, no little kid shapes. There wasn't even a Sugar shape. All the shadows were the same kind—my kind.

As my eyes got used to the dark I saw Bridie, Danny and Mary huddling in one blanket, John, some kids I had never seen before and some things I had never seen before at a bonfire—ends of cigarettes glowing and a giant plastic tub dug into the sand, filled with ice and brown bottles and Cokes and blue and red beer cans. I shot a really quick look at Grandpa, but my grandmother had already tugged him back into the night.

"No one listens to me," he was muttering, and my grandmother turned to whisper to me. "We'll just run along back, dear," she said.

To tell you the truth, for a minute I wished she had said, "I am not going to let you stay down here!" I had friends who tried cigarettes, but I had never been to a party where there had been drinking. Never. Then I said to myself, there's nothing to be afraid of. You've known these kids forever, since as long as Kate, since as long as Grandma and Grandpa. *Montana, I said to myself, are you in there? There is nothing to be afraid of.*

"Erin, you came!" Bridie Kelly shouted at me as I drew closer. An older boy, with this dirty blond hair sticking out from under a railroad cap, sat next to Danny, opening a can of beer that foamed over his hand. Two older girls I had seen in town by the post office once were huddled over on the opposite side of the fire. I remember them because their eyebrows were so thin I decided they had plucked them. Suddenly I felt glad that John Mullin was sitting there, even though he had a can of beer in his hand, too.

All I wanted to do was to fit in, but there was no time to dream up how I was going to do it. How I'd dance over to the bucket and take a beer as if, hey, that's what I did all the time back in big-shot Connecticut. How I'd squeeze in between Danny and Mary and tell Danny how I'd had this crush on him for five years. How I'd tell a great joke no one had ever heard and how they'd all laugh. Because I wasn't *going* to go to some beer party, I was there.

I guess it took me only a few minutes to realize no one even noticed me. Except maybe Bridie Kelly.

"Isn't she pretty?" she said to the boy next to her, pointing at me.

"Look at her hair." She leaned over and ran her fingers down it. "And those eyes, they're like the lake, they're so blue."

Everyone looked at me, *everyone,* and I could have crawled.

Bridie even saw that. "But she's shy, aren't you, Erin?" And she smiled a smile I didn't believe and stroked my cheek. Then she bounced off around the circle, smiling at the boy with the railroad cap and smiling at John who reached up and pulled her down right next to him.

I wanted to crawl somewhere, under the willow tree, under the blanket, anywhere, but I hung in there. I laughed and clapped when they argued the Mullins' Volkswagen was better than the Tracys' Mercedes. I sang when they teased Danny into chugging a quart bottle of some light beer. I was fitting in, just sort of watching the fire turning

41

gray, the edges glowing like miniature apartment build-
ings, when I felt these fingers digging into my shoulders.

"Have a beer, Erin," Bridie whispered into my hair.

Look, a beer is no big deal to me. I'm not afraid of it or
anything. My father has beer in the refrigerator all the
time. He likes it second to martinis, but I didn't want any,
and it was a lot like the bus driver telling me to sit in my
seat. Just tell me I have to do something and I'm a little like
my grandfather.

"No thanks," I said, feeling my cheeks hot.

"Hey, Erin," Mary said from inside the blanket she had
pulled around her and Danny. Mouselike, she had a small
face, small dark eyes and a tight, small voice that never
seemed to say anything original. "Try it, you'll like it,"
she said, echoing some TV advertisement.

I looked across the circle at John for help, but he was
talking to one of the girls with no eyebrows.

"Hey, Olive," Danny leaned over and whispered so that
his warm breath touched my ear. "Go ahead, try it." We
were really old friends and he always called me Olive Oyl
because my legs were so skinny, but to tell you the truth
his voice didn't feel friendly. And for the first time I
thought of Laurie and how much I missed her.

*Denver, where are you? Montana shouted desperately.
It's the Barts! They've surrounded us this time. They're
trampling over us. Over the ponies. Denver, we're going
to lose everything.*

But the truth was, Denver wasn't there.

"No, I really don't want it!" I said, and I started backing
up like a sand crab, pushing myself backward with my
feet.

Bridie didn't even try to stop me. Then I realized she
was signaling the two strangers and grinning, and before I
could get away they sprang at me.

I tried to pull away from the two of them but their arms were strong clamped around mine, and their hands were tight around my wrists and ankles, and all at once I was being carried like a sack across the sand toward the water. I looked up at the upside-down grinning face of the boy with the dirty cap, and I kept trying to laugh and fight at the same time. Then I saw that one of the people carrying a leg was *John Mullin*—and I really kicked.

I don't know why it got so important all of a sudden. Bridie was running alongside, splashing me and shouting. "You're going to get wet one way or the other." I couldn't duck the water she was pouring on me and they were carrying me deeper and deeper into the lake. All at once I felt the guy with the cap stop. Someone's arm looped around his arms—I couldn't see whose—and the top half of me dropped into the water. As I tried to kick myself loose, someone yelled from the shore.

"Let her go!" and I saw Laurie on the shoreline wading toward us.

I struggled against the one hand that was still holding my leg, sort of limping to stay upright in the water with the other, when I saw the boy who had rescued me. It was the boy on the horse. I knew by the shape of his thick shoulders. And he picked up the boy with the railroad cap from behind, lifting him right out of the water.

Suddenly I realized there were teams and I was on one of them, with Laurie. Not two and two, but the boy and Laurie and I made three. Laurie must have told the boy about me just like she said. She hadn't deserted me at all. I struggled to get to my feet and started splashing back and I was still laughing as Laurie's friend dunked the kid in the cap over and over.

Then I heard Bridie rush at him through the water, shouting, "Leave him alone, Matt!" as if this Matt were a bear or something that could only understand if you shouted.

He stopped, letting the boy with the cap pull away into the lake. I guess that was the first time I saw the CALLEY MOTORS written on his T-shirt and knew the boy on the horse and the boy on the motorcycle and the person on my team were the same person. I looked up at the bluff wondering if my grandfather were watching freighters with his binoculars in this direction when Bridie suddenly brushed past me and, laughing, tackled the boy with the railroad cap.

Water flew around them as they plunged, laughing, deeper and deeper into the lake and they dodged around me as if I were only a spectator, or some kind of china doll they didn't want to break. But I didn't care because Denver had come through! The boy she loved had saved me. And, dripping wet, I waded in toward them and the three of us stood together by this great, flaming bonfire, our arms touching. It was better than I could have dreamed.

"I saw you on the beach," I admitted, looking up at Laurie. "Riding."

Laurie brushed her hair back and looked at Matt.

"I mean, it looked like a lot of fun," I said really quickly because I didn't want them to think I had seen anything private.

She seemed sort of relieved. "It is fun, Erin."

The three of us stood there without saying anything for a minute, and I was so afraid they'd go.

"Missy's a nice horse," I added, hoping that was enough to keep them.

"She is, Erin. You ought to have a horse, shouldn't she, Matt? You could come riding with us, Erin."

"I could?" I hoped I didn't sound like an eager Nellie,

which is what my father calls me when I get too excited too soon.

Laurie looked at Matt who was not exactly looking at me. "Sure," he said.

"Wait a minute . . . there's the Luddy horse," Laurie said, "that old black gelding. No one rides it anymore and he's kind of wild, but"—I shrugged and laughed a little— "well, you could try him, Erin. I'd come with you."

"Would you, Laurie?"

Matt had put his arm on hers and pulled away slightly, I could see that even in the dark, but we were a team and so I said, "How about tomorrow, how about one o'clock?" and she nodded and Matt put both of his arms around her neck and kissed the back of the hair by her ear. But I didn't mind him kissing her hair because now I knew that liking him was liking Laurie and liking Laurie was liking him.

"By Sugar's driveway?" I said and she nodded.

I had forgotten all about my grandfather, but when I turned to sit down, feeling so good and warm that I was sure that it showed on my face, I saw this shadow with a captain's hat stoop under the tree and start toward the bonfire. It was Grandpa.

He practically ran across the circle, and I knew I wanted to disappear before he said a word. "You, Calley Motors," he said to Matt, his voice shakier than I had ever heard it. I think I remembered every story he had ever told me about the Fairview Kid in that second, about how he could out-run any kid on the street even though he was only five feet tall. How even six-foot Butch Miller was afraid of the Fairview Kid, he was so strong. A tough Depression kid.

"You have a motorcycle?" he asked.

"Yeah, I have a bike," Matt said, his lower lip tightening as he got to his feet.

45

"You run across my pipe?"

"Not really. I've made a few runs down the beach," Calley said sort of bitterly.

"The pipe's on my beach."

"Wrong, ten feet from the water is everybody's beach." The boy was so close he was like a taller shadow of my grandfather. But thicker.

"The pumphouse is more than ten feet from the water!" my grandfather said and gave Calley a shove which sent him staggering backward across the sand, and John jumped to his feet.

"Mr. Lawton!" he said, but my grandfather had already grabbed Matt by his two collars. I couldn't believe it, I wasn't brought up on Fairview Avenue, and I started pulling on the back of my grandfather's shirt and saying "Grandpa!" when I realized I was hearing something.

I don't know what I heard first, the waves starting to pick up as if the weather were changing or the bell ringing in the pumphouse, but the minute my grandfather heard the bell, he let go of the boy's shirt.

"Bridie!" someone shouted from the top of the bluff near the Kellys'. "Laurie, Danny, Bridie! What's that bell?" Then they must have seen the waves. "You kids get up here! There's going to be a storm!"

My grandfather turned and pounded across the sand toward the pumphouse which was between the bonfire and our steps. Matt lurched at him, but John and Danny just pulled him back, folding his arms behind him. The bell kept ringing, the waves were getting louder, and the other kids scrambled to pull the beer cans out of the ice-packed bucket and scoop up the blankets.

"What's the bell going off for?" my grandpa barked, as he stalked off into the dark.

"Boy, Erin," Bridie said as she scooped up her blankets

46

in her arms and started past me too. "You sure know how to mess things up."

I handle a lot of things. Like Kate. Like a seventy-year-old grandfather who thinks he's seventeen even. But this wasn't so easy to handle because I knew I couldn't have really messed things up. Laurie would know that if no one else would, and I turned toward the bonfire to find her, but she was gone. The two of them had disappeared into the dark. So I turned and started to walk toward the stairs alone, trying to catch up to my grandmother, when a shadow shouted ahead at me.

"Need a light?" John Mullin said, aiming the beam in front of me.

"No," I said, struggling to get across the soft sand. I didn't want anything from him ever.

"Mr. Lawton?" he called ahead to my grandfather, who had reached the pumphouse and was trying to open the door.

"No, John, no," my grandfather said as he fumbled with the handle, and I saw John run back alone toward his beach.

"Grandma," I whispered when I finally caught up to her, "why's the bell ringing?"

I could feel my grandmother shrug.

"Grandma, did you do something to it?"

She didn't answer for a moment. "Well, I may have tripped over the pipe on my way to the fire and disconnected it," she said. "I'm so clumsy sometimes."

I wondered. But she started toward the pumphouse with that soft, round chin right out in front of her. Sometimes my grandmother reminds me of a tiny plump robin and sometimes of an army sergeant.

I was panting as hard as my grandma when I reached the top of the stairs and found my grandfather with his binoculars already looking across the dark lake where clouds had blocked out the moon.

"Grandpa, why did you do that to Laurie's friend?" I said to him. "Couldn't you just talk? Did you have to push and shout? Did you have to ruin everything?"

He didn't say anything back. He just lowered his binoculars as if someone had knocked them away from his eyes.

Six

All night it rained, the waves shushing up on the shore tearing at the bluff, and my grandfather paced in the room next to my room, and my grandmother got up and paced with him. I swear he was enjoying that storm.

But I didn't get up with them because I was wrapped up thinking Matt had helped me! Probably he liked me because Laurie had told him all about me. And maybe now the three of us would do everything together, go to town, hang out at the General Store, ride. And the next time they rode down on the beach and splashed and laughed as the horses danced through the water, I'd ride my horse and splash, too. Everyone would get used to seeing the three of us together. "Those three!" they'd whisper.

All at once I realized why the motorcycle was spending so much time in front of our cottage—it wasn't Grandpa at all. We lived near Laurie. And Grandpa thought it was all for him! Was he wrong! He was probably wrong about Matt running through the tomato garden, too.

The sun had risen to the center of this bowl of Michigan sky when I reached the driveway of Sugar's farm at ten to one the next day. I sat on a rock facing the road so I would be able to see her coming. I even liked watching Laurie walk with those big long legs.

You're going after a real horse this time, Montana! I said out loud. Then I quick looked around to see if anyone heard me.

I kept watching the road and wiping my forehead with a blue paisley bandana I had brought along, but Laurie didn't come and didn't come. And I knew it must be after one and my insides began to hurt when the road kept being empty. Then I saw John riding up the road with a roll of wire on the back of this little mud bike, his knees bowing out like a stork on a fence, and I hated seeing him because in a funny way I was thinking if he hadn't come, Laurie would have. I pretended I hadn't even seen him and started walking down the road toward the Luddys'.

"Hey," he called out. "Want a ride?"

"I'm waiting for Laurie."

"Seems like you're always waiting for Laurie." He grinned.

"Seems like she's got a horse to take care of now!"

As he started pedaling his bike out ahead of me, I could see he was having trouble keeping the wire on, but I didn't help and when he was up a good way, he dragged his feet. "Sure you don't want a ride?" he asked.

I shook my head no.

"Look, you're not doing anything."

"I'm going to see about the Luddy horse." I got out and realized that now I would have to make good my claim, whether Laurie came or not. But he got a funny expression on his face.

"The Luddy horse!" he said almost as if he didn't like that for some reason, but then he sort of dropped it.

"You got a dunking last night," he said sheepishly, pedaling real slow beside me.

"A drowning, you mean."

"We were just messing around. You weren't scared, were you? I mean, I almost thought you got scared."

"You never get scared?" I asked.

"Not much," he answered.

"Well, I wasn't scared either. I just prefer being with more mature people, that's all."

"Like Laurie and Matt, for instance."

"Like Laurie and Matt, for instance," I repeated.

He was trailing behind me, holding the wire on with his one hand. When I looked back, I decided he had big ears. It was all very well to have shoulders like a gymnast, but his ears looked as if he could fly.

"Well, I don't know how mature I am, but, well, I've worked the Luddy fences and I've seen Luddy fight with that animal and maybe it's just crazy Luddy, but, well, I don't know if anyone can ride that horse," he said, dragging his feet to keep his bike from falling over. "Maybe I can help."

"Catch a horse?" I asked.

"Catch anything," he said.

"Well, I don't need your help," I said. "Laurie will meet me there."

"Why don't you give up on her, Erin?"

"She'll meet me there." I could feel my face burning and probably leaving blotches on my face, which I really hate.

"Whatever Bridie Kelly does is not good. Whatever Laurie Kelly does is okay."

"Laurie's not doing anything."

"She's not meeting you."

"She will," I said. I just knew that she would this time.

"She won't. She's with Calley."

"She's with Missy!" I guess I didn't say anything for a second, but then I added, "In the far field—working out."

He threw a quick glance back at the field which even I could see was empty and said, "All right, all right. I'm coming with you anyway."

"Don't," I said.

"I am." He threw the wire down on the side of the road and started pedaling next to me but I purposely started walking where the sand was thick and he would have trouble keeping his bike upright. He followed me anyway.

At the Luddy farm, Mrs. Luddy had been canning pickles and her dark kitchen smelled strong like vinegar and cloves and I could hardly see her through the screen door when I asked if I could borrow her old riding horse. The wooden floor squeaked as she walked across it with some kind of big black dog behind her. "I don't mind, but I ain't takin' no responsibility," she said. "You understand that. You want the horse, you catch it. You saddle it. You get on it. Hear?"

I pressed my face to the screen. A heavy, round sort of woman—around thirty or so—with her hair pulled back, she went into a back room and came out holding a lead rope with a metal hook on the end. A black-faced German shepherd sniffed the screen and growled. "The horse's got a halter on him," she said. "He shouldn't be hard to catch. His name is Shadow."

"Thank you, Ma'am," I said to her politely.

John stood out in the driveway straddling his bike with his arms crossed and his head cocked as if he doubted I could do it, but of course that was all I needed. I took the lead rope she handed to me through the crack in the door.

"I ain't takin' no responsibility," the woman said again.

I turned toward the stairs which tipped weirdly to the left. The house was real old, a two-story red brick with pretty carved wood like lace in the roofline.

"Oh, watch the geese," the woman called out to me as I started down the walk, "and if you see Leon, don't pay him no mind." I guessed Leon was her husband. Crazy Luddy, John had called him.

The barn was more of a skeleton of a barn than the real thing. Slats were missing in the sides and roof, showing the blue sky behind it. I almost thought the barn had been burned out except, as I walked closer, I could see the siding was more gray than black and looked something like a beached ark that was sinking into a field of weeds.

As I walked through the weeds, waist high, I swear I never heard the geese until I saw them.

But all of a sudden, their necks sticking out, beaks open, hissing, twenty of them came swarming like giant insects down the driveway after us. Even John turned with this kind of horrified expression on his face.

"Run to the barn," he shouted as he scooped up an old rusty coffee can, but, spotting a broken feed pail in the weeds, I picked it up and threw it at them. John threw the can, too, but the geese just scattered for seconds and came swarming at us again.

We began running, but the running just seemed to get them excited, and they flew after us, their necks out, hissing as if they were furious at us for putting a foot in their field. The barnyard fence was as broken down as the barn but I straddled the broken top rail, then flipped over and John jumped after me, throwing a glass Coke bottle at the hissing birds.

My ears were ringing when I sank against the barn siding, and John sank next to me, his warm shoulder touching mine.

"You want to hear something?" he said.

"Yes," I panted.

"I was scared."

And I looked at him, biting my cheeks on the inside and nodding. "Ah-huh!" I said, and he threw his head back against the barn.

"Yep, scared." We started to laugh.

"And we were worried about the horse," I said, and I felt the two o'clock sun hot on my face.

And we just sat together like that for a few minutes, sort of smiling and feeling the sun, when I spotted this movement out in the back of the barnyard. It had to be Shadow, standing on a narrow trail that wound out a back gateway between a small pond and another fence.

"Shadow," I whispered and sat up straighter, watching. He had a smallish head for his tall body but a rubbery chin that he kind of pushed out in front of him as if he were daring anyone to come near him. Or as if he had won the Kentucky Derby in other years and now deserved to retire. He didn't look old, though, he did look mean.

"And I thought the geese were bad," I must have muttered.

"He's all right," John whispered, but he didn't move either. "We can take him."

But I suddenly looked around at him. He didn't understand at all. "No," I said. "What I mean is, I'll catch him. Laurie's coming and . . ."

"Look, Erin, Laurie's been coming and coming. Right? Well, you know what? I don't see her." He stood up and wiped his mouth with the back of his hand. "Get real, Erin!" he said and I stood up too and was trying to find some words to say to him when he turned his back on me,

54

crouched under the broken slat and hiked toward the
house. At the lane he grabbed his bike which he had leaned
against this big maple tree and, running, jumped on it and
pedaled right past the hissing geese out to the road.

"*What's real, John?*" I shouted after him, but he
had already turned onto Ratt, and, as I watched him
pedal away, I thought, all right, if he wants to go, let
him.

I turned around, slowly, facing the giant horse. He was
going to be problem enough, I thought to myself. Then, I
thought, I just have to do what I've seen Sugar do. That's
all. And I drew closer and closer, the lead rope in my hand,
but that was a mistake. Seeing the rope, the horse suddenly stopped and just stood there like a giant black deer,
its head frozen, but its eyes watching everything.

As I moved closer, its nostrils moved slightly and its
black tail whisked from one side to the other flagging the
flies away, but its legs stood firm, as if they were locked.
He was a giant animal, his shoulders really high, his head
up as if he were a king here. King of the empty pasture.
King of the broken-down barn. King of the weeds. But
king, for sure.

His nostrils twitched and his dark eyes darted to the
side.

I drew closer though the top of me didn't move at all.
"Easy, boy," I heard myself saying as I had heard Sugar
say so many times. All I had to do was grab a small ring at
the side of the horse's jaw where the three parts of the
halter met.

"Easy . . ."

Step by slow step, I drew closer. When I was within
arm's reach, I suddenly reached out, but it was as if my
hands didn't really want to catch him, and sensing it and
seeing the lead rope, he sprang backwards and, lurching

sideways, turned and galloped away down the weedy path by the pond.

I sat down on a dried rut of mud in the middle of the yard watching the underside of his hooves as he disappeared down the path. "Oh, Denver," I suddenly said out loud, "why didn't you come?"

Seven

I don't remember ever being mad at Laurie. Ever since I was three and she was six I had trailed around after her as if she were a second mother or something. When she said, "Let's build a hideout in the woods," I started running for wood. When she said, "Let's make popcorn" in the middle of the night, I started melting the butter. Even when we rode the beach, whatever she saw, I saw. If it was the Barts coming down the ravine, I started shooting. If she said my pony had come up lame, I started limping.

But by the time I had outrun the geese to get back on the road that day, I decided I was a little crazy to be running around after a big, mean horse for someone who didn't care about me. If Laurie had cared, she would have met me or come to the Luddy farm. Something.

I still might have talked myself out of that, but when I started hiking past Sugar's barn I saw the black and silver motorcycle parked out in back of the manure pile and saw Missy grazing in the field as if she hadn't been ridden in a month. The barn door was shut.

I started adding everything up, and what I added up was

that Laurie Kelly didn't care about me. Her head was so full of Matt, she wasn't seeing clear, and if she wanted to pick Matt Calley over me, fine. I could be stubborn. I wouldn't have to outrun any geese or junkyard, or any giant horse either, because I wasn't going to go back to the Luddys' again.

I'm sure for the next week my grandparents must have thought I had really turned into the perfect child. I did dishes, I swept, I helped my grandmother take the stitching out of a pocket she had sewn shut by mistake. I still hadn't talked to my grandfather since the night of the bonfire, but I cleaned the spark plugs of his old Dodge car. Oh, and I swam a lot, sunbathed alone out in the lake on Whale Rock.

I heard Bridie and her gang down on the beach one night, and I think they may have called out "Erin," but it was almost as if someone shushed whoever had called out. Not that I wanted to go anywhere with Bridie Kelly and her friends. Any of them.

Of course my grandmother noticed, and sort of offhand when she was changing sheets one night and the kids were noising off over at the Mullins', she said, "You going with those kids tonight?"

"No," I said.

"But why, dear?"

"I really don't know them anymore."

"Oh."

"Do you think I'm right not to go, Grandma?"

Throwing the dirty sheets in a pile, she sat down next to me and took my hands in her hands, as if her hands would be able to say something her words couldn't.

"I think you have to find out what's right for you, Erin, what people are right for you. You'll know when that

58

happens." She brushed my hair back like she used to when I was ten, and it felt good.

I waited for a few seconds. "Have you ever thought about 'real,' Gram?" I wasn't sure why John's saying, "Get real," bothered me. I mean, it was only slang.

"Not so much, dear," she said. "Isn't everything real when you get down to it?" .

"Not dreams."

"Well, that's true enough."

"Not ideas."

"Oh, I'm not so sure about that, sweetie." She stood and reached up into the closet for the clean sheets and I could smell them like fresh air.

"I think the Luddys' geese are real. More real than ideas. Or dreams," I said.

"Oh," she said, as if she had discovered something.

"And the dust on Ratt Road after the cars go by and farmers' dogs . . . and once I saw a cat run over by a truck near Sugar's, bleeding in his ear."

"Ah, you think things that hurt are real, geese, cars, dogs, the cat on the road. Is that what you've run into when you've gone across the highway? Hmmmm, maybe you think it's more real over there?" She put her soft arms around me and squeezed me and we laughed.

"But, Gram . . . maybe that's not so silly. Maybe it is more real across the highway."

She flicked out the sheet—it had small faded yellow flowers that I remember forever—and she smiled at me as if she could say more but wasn't quite ready.

"Or maybe it's just that I'm not very brave." My grandma looked up at me as if to say "nonsense." "No, Grandma, I'm not!"

"Maybe you just haven't had reason."

59

"Maybe." I pulled the corner tight.

She waited for a moment. "How are you and Laurie?" she asked.

"I'm not playing with Laurie anymore," I answered and, as I finished making square corners, she pulled the crocheted quilt someone's grandmother had made over the end of the bed.

"For a week, a month, . . . a lifetime?" She grinned.

"I mean it, Grandma."

"I believe you, dear, I believe you."

"Sometimes it's just easier not to see a person again."

"Well, you may be right, Erin, but then . . ."

"I think I am right, Grandma."

My grandfather and I started talking the next day. It was an afternoon when these thick storm clouds hung over the lake like a shelf. Below them there were three freighters that looked as if they had somehow steamed out of the freighter lanes in the middle of the lake and might collide. Grandpa refused to leave the porch, even though dinner was on.

"That's silly," my grandmother said to him. "What good are you going to do those freighters if you sit there and let your dinner get cold?"

"It's not the freighters," he snapped back at her. "It's the storm."

"Now you're going to wait for every storm that hits the lake? You'll starve," Grandma said from the kitchen.

"There are storms and storms."

"You'll starve," she repeated without coming out.

"Maybe you think there couldn't be another big one? Is that what you think, Ethel?" he said to the empty door-way.

I waited expecting him to go on about the "big one," but he didn't, so I just asked him, plain out.

"What 'big one,' Grandpa?"

He didn't exactly look at me, but—miracle!—he did start talking.

"November 8, 1913 . . . ," he began, and stopped as if his motor had run down.

"Yes . . . ?"

"We still had partial rigs on the lake then, you know, a kind of mixture between a sailing board and a full steam, all steaming up and down these lakes. But that day the sky turned gun-metal gray. Weather reports just said rain, just said west to southwest winds."

I watched my grandpa's face and waited, but he had stopped again. "Yes, Grandpa, yes?"

"Well, it got quiet, the way it does before any storm, then the wind swung to the northeast, and two storm fronts met. Eighty miles an hour across the lake the wind came. But here's the fooler, the wind swung *again. And again.*" He had gripped the arms of the lawn chair as if he had a seat by the rail of an ocean steamer. "Around and around like a clock gone crazy."

I leaned forward in the rocker, tucking my feet under waiting for the next part. "Then?"

He looked out at the three freighters that were even closer to each other now. "Waves thirty-five feet high struck the ships, wiped out the pilothouses, broke mast-heads, swept off deckhouses. Beams thrown hundreds of miles. Men washed overboard. More than forty ships went down . . . over two hundred men . . . drowned."

Then he kind of paused and whispered under his breath and looked right at me for the first time in a long time. "Like a giant *tornado.*"

"Here," he really insisted, pushing the binoculars into my hands. "Look."

"At the storm?" I asked.

"No, at the freighters," he said impatiently, and for the first time when I looked through the binoculars I saw more than my eyelashes. I could see a big ocean freighter and could see that it was nowhere near the lake ship it looked as if it were going to hit.

"I can see it!" I said and my grandpa grinned at me. "With the binoculars!"

"Of course, you can! You've got my genes, haven't you?" He put his hands on my shoulders. "Now tell me what you see."

"Well, I think it's Swedish, with the loaders in the center. . . ."

"Right, so far."

"Not storing oil, not enough room." All the things he had ever told me were coming to me and I screwed the focus to get a better look.

"And . . . it's diesel."

"Right," my grandfather purred.

"That's all," I said.

"Nope," he said smugly and his unlit cigar jiggled between his lips. "Twin engine, too."

"Oh," I said and, as if we had solved a mystery together, we both sat on the bank and watched the faraway ships go by, entirely missing each other. I think we both forgot we hadn't been speaking.

But I didn't smell any storm the way my grandpa did, and he was right again. That night while I was lying in bed, I heard the birch tree outside on the bluff. Since before I could remember I would listen to it at night, sort of whispering, reminding me it was there. But that night, the whisper broke into something breathy and the lake started

62

up and I could hear it slapping at the bluff. I thought, no wonder my grandfather worried about the little pumphouse with a lake that could get so stirred up it could swallow forty giant ships and two hundred men, and then I thought, but that was a long time ago. Even though the waves rolled into the bluff even now, storms like that don't happen anymore.

I had nearly dropped off to sleep that night listening to the wind and the trees when the telephone rang. Automatically, I pushed off the covers and ran through the doorway and down the stairs, grabbing the phone in the dark before it could ring again.

"That you, Erin?" It was Laurie, for the first time, it was Laurie.

"Yes, Laurie," I said, "it's me," and I looked at the ship clock on the desk. The green numbers glowed ten o'clock, but I didn't care. I knew Laurie was calling to say she was sorry she hadn't come to the Luddys', sorry she had waited so many days before calling, sorry we hadn't had a chance to talk.

"How's Matt?" I burst out, because the truth was, I still wanted to be with the two of them. They were my team and I wanted to splash through the waves with them. Laugh with them.

"He's fine," she said, and there was a pause.

"Maybe I'll ride Shadow over," I said, and I had no idea where those words came from.

"Shadow?" she asked.

"The Luddy horse," I said.

"Oh, sure, ah . . . the Luddy horse."

For a minute I almost thought she didn't remember, but I knew that couldn't be it so I kept on. "Maybe we can ride down on the beach."

"Sure, Erin, sometime let's do that."

There was a very long pause and I nearly said something again, but she started before I could. "Grandma Kelly's kind of crazy, Erin, everytime there's a storm, she bakes . . . and, well, . . . can we borrow some baking soda?"

"Oh, sure . . . ," I said.

"I mean, I know it's late, just put the box outside on the porch," she said.

". . . Sure, that's what I'll do," I said. "I'll just put it outside on the porch."

I tried to tiptoe past my grandparents' door because I really didn't want to have to talk to my grandma, but she called out.

"Who was it, Erin?"

"Oh . . . just the Kellys."

There was a pause, then the bed creaked, "What do they want?"

"Baking soda."

"That's all?"

"Yes," I said, "that's all."

Eight

Next morning I didn't tell my grandparents exactly where I was going when I saw them pulling the wagon across the beach to repair some damage the storm had done to the pumphouse door the night before. I just kind of waved off from the top of the bluff. After telling my grandma it was easier never to see Laurie again, I wasn't ready to tell her a day later I had changed my mind and was going to the Luddys' to train Shadow so Matt and Laurie and I could be three and three. After I caught that horse and trained him and ran him until he was sweaty, maybe then I'd tell her where I had been going mornings. And maybe I'd tell her how if Laurie ever wanted me, I had to go.

Other summers I used to think Steffie waited at her window for me to go somewhere, so I wasn't surprised when I started down Ratt Road that day and saw her flying out of her cottage and down the long driveway to catch up. Her pigtails had just been braided and she had on a clean blue-plaid blouse with a smear of red raspberry jam across her cheek and a milk mustache, and, wearing white sneakers without socks, she kept scratching at a strip of poison ivy that ran in bumps down the back of her leg.

"Where you going, Montana?" she asked, scratching, her eyes still sleepy.

"The name's Erin," I said.

"Okay, where you going, Erin." Nothing discouraged that kid.

"To catch a horse," I told her.

"John can't come."

"I didn't ask him to come."

"He's going with Bridie and Mary and Danny to the Crosly Fairgrounds. The fair's opening in *three days,* and I wanted to go, but they didn't want me to come with them—I think they want to be *alone.*" She mugged. "Anyhow I'd rather catch a horse with you."

"Steffie, I really don't care where they're going, do you care?"

"No, Erin," she said, "I don't care."

"Good," I said and walked ahead of her, but for some crazy reason I let her come even though I knew she'd just be in the way.

Sugar was jumping Missy in the front field when we walked by, and when I told her I was going to catch old Shadow, she said I needed some oats and molasses for that and she told me to go get a bucketful.

"Just shake it to catch him," she said. I didn't know exactly what she meant but I nodded.

"You can do it, Montana," she said and put her heels into Missy to move on. I didn't mind if Sugar called me that.

At the Luddy farm I waved at Mrs. Luddy through the screen and never did see Mr. Luddy that day, though I picked up chicken feed at the Luddys' poultry house, this ramshackle old shed that someone must have built with a left hand. I had a plan to handle those geese, and when they began to swarm at me and Steffie at the end of the driveway, I threw the feed onto the road in front of the little monsters. All of them whipped their necks around to get that seed, except one big gray honker, probably the daddy of them all. I heard once a goose could break your leg with his neck. Well, in a second he lost interest in the seed, and he came after our legs. When I saw him, I started to run through those weeds with Steffie screaming after me, and neither of us stopped until we made the fence. Those hissers piled up outside the broken-down gate, mad as hornets.

But no one—or nothing—was going to stop me that day. I was going to get on that horse.

I found Shadow hiding under a threshing bay inside the barn to escape the morning sun. His tail whisked as flies buzzed over his back. He looked just as mean, and when I tiptoed over the old manure that had dried into sort of a seedy carpet, his ears twitched back. But I fooled him. I didn't go after him this time. I did what Sugar had said to do. With that pail in my hand, I stood by the side of the barn and just shook it, rattling the oats and molasses against the sides, and not moving one inch.

He swung his head slowly around and gave the pail a maybe look.

"Easy," I cooed softly and shook the pail again. I figured he didn't have to know how I felt scared inside, and he looked at the pail once more, then slowly he just turned and walked across the dark doorway toward the pail and me. When he nudged his nose into the bucket, I grabbed the halter ring and clipped the lead rope on him.

I could hardly believe it.

"All right, Steffie, I'm going to get the saddle," I said. "Stay out of the way." If catching the horse was so easy, the saddle had to be a breeze.

The barn was creepy, I remember that now, and the saddle, a thick western one with a pommel that stuck up like a turkey's head, sat on a wooden horse covered with dusty cobwebs in a corner of the old barn with the bridle looped over it. It was so dark I could hardly see the fancy scrawled design on the sideflaps until I stood right next to it.

But even standing next to it, I could hardly lift it. Finally, though, I propped the leather monster against my stomach and managed to carry it out to the fence where Shadow was tied. I'd get the bridle later, I decided, just glad to be out in the light again.

When the horse saw me coming, he turned his muscly bottom at me and went on tearing at a weed that grew up around the split post he was tied to.

Some of the cobwebs had stuck to my arms and when I reached up to wipe the sweat dripping from my cheeks, cobwebs stuck on my nose. "Wipe my nose, Steffie," I said, leaning backward to balance the dumb saddle on my stomach with both hands.

Steffie pinched the cobweb off, and Shadow shifted again, pulling against the rope. He really was a big horse. All I could smell was him.

"Just stay out of the way, runt," I said to Steffie.

First I piled the stirrups on top of the seat and tried to lift the saddle like I'd lift a suitcase, but it was clumsy, and I had raised it to somewhere near the horse's ribs when it slipped down his side onto the ground. I sank down with it. Then I caught sight of this gray concrete block and I dragged the block over to the fence.

Leaning way back, I picked up the saddle and propped it

on my stomach again, then slowly felt for the concrete block with my toe and inched on it. Settling myself there, I angled the saddle onto the horse's side, and started shoving it upward.

But I could just feel it fighting back.

"Steffie!" I yelled, "I need a new grip!"

She scrambled under the saddle and with the stirrups on her head, one draped across her eyes, she pushed up and I regripped and started pushing up too. The two of us had the saddle almost onto the horse's back when suddenly Shadow reared against the rope and the saddle slipped over Steffie's head, pulling both of us to the ground with it.

"Quitting?" she asked me, her fingertips covered with barnyard dust.

I just looked at her. "No!"

"Well, I'd quit."

"Well, I'm not you, Steffie." I was really mad at that saddle. "And you can go home if you want."

But she didn't move.

"All right, Steffie," I said, real soft, "I've got an idea. Shorten the rope and keep Shadow pinned against the fence so he can't move."

Steffie nodded and, spanking off her dusty hands on her dirty shorts, she climbed the fence and shortened the rope while I planted the palms of both my hands squarely against Shadow's gut and pushed him up to the side of the fence.

"Get over, you big tank," I said, between my teeth. "Now, keep him here, Stef," I shouted, and I pulled her off the fence and put her hands right where I wanted them on Shadow's belly.

"I got 'im, Erin!" she said.

"Good!" Then quick I dragged the concrete block over

and when Shadow started to dance back over the block, I slapped him one on the rear.

"Behave!" I said. "You think you can push me around? You think I'm nobody or something? Well, think again, Horse!"

And I picked up the saddle in the middle, and stood on the concrete block. "Now, Steffie!" I was practically shouting, but the two of us pushed that saddle up the side of the horse and we pushed until I had a mustache of sweat. When the saddle was finally near the top, I shouted, *"Yes! Yes!"* and Steffie pinned it there while I ran around and, climbing the fence on the other side, pulled it across the top of his back by the stirrups.

"You got it, Erin. You got it!" she shouted, as if the saddle were the wild animal instead of the horse.

For a minute, I just leaned my forehead against the saddle. Man, I whispered to myself. I had sweat running salty into my mouth. I wished my dad could have seen that, and Queen Kate and all her friends. Maybe even my mom. I grinned under the horse at Steffie.

"You did good, runt," I said, probably sounding a lot like Laurie used to sound to me.

"I know it, Montana."

"Erin!"

"I know, I know," she said, hunching her neck into her shoulders and grinning.

When I noticed it was already eleven o'clock I knew we had fought that saddle for almost an hour. I had promised to get home by noon and wouldn't be getting on Shadow today, but somehow, crazy as it seemed, that was okay.

Just as I was thinking that, Shadow swung his head around and bit my arm which was still resting on his side.

70

"Damn!" I said, and swatted him one right on the rear. "You do that again, Horse, and you're dead!"

Steffie looked up at me as if she had just run into Frankenstein.

"Don't you see, Steffie, you just can't let them be boss."

Nine

The first day Jim Anders, Littleton's one patrolman, came to the cottage, we hadn't even had breakfast, and when I looked through the door he had his thick, big knuckled hand on his gun.

"Someone's really hit the cottage side this time," Jim said when he saw Grandpa come down the stairs in his brown bathrobe with his legs sticking down below like chicken's legs. "Boozed it up in Scranton's boat house, then battered his new Evinrude motor hanging down from the beam. Left empty bottles all over."

"Not surprised," my grandpa said, looking at me, and the minute Anders left he ran down to check the pumphouse. I thought, he is really paranoid, but this time he found something. The pumphouse door had been sprung open and inside in a corner there was a crumpled red flannel shirt that someone had left behind.

"Those two," he muttered when he came slowly up the stairs, "they'd sneak into any empty shed."

I knew the "they" he was hinting about were Matt and Laurie and what he was hinting about was disgusting. And unfair. "I don't know what you mean!" I said to him, not too softly.

"I'm not dumb," he said. "A little beer here, a nice empty pumphouse there. These beach places are real convenient for kids' messing around, that's what they are, real convenient."

"That isn't fair, Grandpa," I broke in, "you don't know if that shirt was Matt's—I never saw him in a red shirt! And you don't know if Laurie was there with him, you don't know that at all!" I said and I was practically screaming it when he turned his back on me and walked out the kitchen door toward his tool shed.

The news about the Scrantons' motor and the shirt in Grandpa's pumphouse spread right down the bluff from cottage to cottage. Burning rolls of hay, even running over tomato plants were one thing. Breaking in was something else. My grandmother called the Tracys, and the patrolman stopped to tell the Kellys, though Grandpa said he didn't know why since Laurie Kelly would just tip off Calley Motors that the police were after him. It seemed like the whole bluff got jittery after that, wondering where who-ever-it-was would strike next.

I did wonder who it was, but I knew it wasn't Laurie, and I didn't even think it was Matt Calley.

Anyway, that was when my grandfather really started fortifying the pumphouse. First he finished circling the place with more rocks—it looked a lot like a nest of giant eggs—then he repainted the pumphouse a deep red color to match the cottage and put up extra wooden beams inside it. Finally he put the wire fence up around it and a lock on the door though he said he just *ought* to let *someone* get in since *someone* who didn't know the pump could electrocute himself pretty easy and that would serve *someone* right.

73

Anyway, when it was finished, what it reminded me of was a gatehouse of one of those mansions stuck back in the woods in Connecticut that I knew were there, but that I never saw because all I saw was the gatehouse guarding the road.

When my grandfather finally decided the pumphouse was done, he started guarding it. Some afternoons he'd sneak his shotgun, binoculars and a lawn chair down there and I'd see him sort of stationed on the little concrete apron that stuck out around the tin building, all by himself. No one was going to get into his pumphouse again, not while he was there! I suspect he watched freighters to pass the time, but he never called me down to see the tanker *Cort* or a Swedish twin diesel or to talk about a storm while he was doing it. The truth was, after our shouting match about the red shirt, my grandfather must have decided I was on the other side of the crack with Matt and Laurie, and he stopped talking to me altogether again.

"Is he ever going to forgive me?" I asked my grandmother one day when he had started down the beach stairs alone with his newspaper tucked under his arm without even looking at me as he passed. I thought he was acting pretty dumb.

"Just give him some time, dear. This mood'll blow over. His moods always do," she said as if she were describing a storm.

Anyway, Steffie and I had our own little pattern every morning. Early, we'd meet at the highway and start down Ratt. At Sugar's we'd drop off John's lunch where he was working on the fences. (We had had nothing to say to each other either since he had followed me to the Luddys' that day.) Then we'd pick up the oats and molasses, and head down road for the Luddys'.

Sometimes Mrs. Luddy would follow us out and watch

us from the rail fence. I don't think she had enough to do. Someone said she had lost a baby when she was practically just a girl herself and she never had any more, and she complained a lot about Mr. Luddy and his leaving bottles in the lawn or going off in his truck instead of catching the chickens that kept getting through the tear in the fence. I only saw him once at all, watching us from the barn loft, and I couldn't figure out exactly what he was doing up there since the loft was as full of holes as the sides of the barn and it could barely have held a bale of hay, let alone a big man.

Anyway, I finally mounted Shadow and after that every day I'd walk or trot him around and around the inside field. I can't say I liked Shadow, even then, not exactly anyway. We could just stand each other a little better. But I knew I had to take him outside the barnyard into the open field if I ever wanted to ride with Laurie.

Since the week had gone so well, I decided the next Monday would be the perfect day. But that morning Steffie wasn't at the Y in the road and she was a little like Shadow, I didn't exactly love her, but I had gotten used to her and I doubled back to her cottage.

"I can't come, Erin!" She had caught poison ivy and all she could do was call from the couch on her front porch. I could hear her scratching from the rear door. "Take John's lunch!"

I had a feeling it wasn't going to be my day, and I was right. By the time I got close to Sugar's the mist had turned to a soft rain, nothing sweeping or stormy but wet. I ran all the way down the driveway to the barn. Then the flies were terrible. I kept swatting them and a giant horse-fly bit my hand so hard that when I slapped it, I couldn't knock it off. I tried to scoop up the molasses and oats, but they stuck together, and when I put my hand in to break them up, they stuck to my hand. Just to top things off, the water spigot in the barn wouldn't turn and all the horses' pails were empty.

I turned to look for John and couldn't even see him along the fence, so I threw his lunch on the feed barrel and started down the driveway right in the rain. It was soft and warm, but really wet, and it ran into my eyes and my mouth. When I got to the end of the driveway, I saw him over by the front ring, pulling nails out of a shed that some wind had turned over. He had taken off his shirt and the rain was rolling down his broad back in beads as if he were greased or something, and his jeans were getting drenched.

"Your lunch is in the barn," I called out.

He glanced up, sort of surprised, then squinted at me and started pulling at some nail or something.

"Okay," was all he said.

For a minute, I stopped, then decided if that was all he was going to say, that was okay with me, and I started to walk away.

But then he shouted, "You're not riding today," without looking up.

"Yes, I am," I shouted back.

"Too wet," was what he said.

"*You're* working in the rain," I said. "Why shouldn't I ride?" though it wasn't any place for another argument.

"Try the porch," he said.

"I'll do what I want to do, John!" I said.

"I know that," he said and he laughed even though he went on working.

"You just don't want me to go to the Luddys' without Steffie. Right? What do you think, Mrs. Luddy will pickle me?" I keep imagining my own silly jokes and the thought of me in a jar with my fingers pressed against the glass was

76

pretty outrageous. "Or Crazy Luddy will catch me and put me in his chicken coop?"

Honestly, I don't know what made me say that.

I looked up at the sky and licked the rain off my lips, then, deciding it wouldn't exactly be giving in, I ran over to the porch. Even though it was warm, I was shaking. I sat there alone for a few minutes. He didn't make one move to come out of the rain himself, and I sat and sat and started to think I didn't have to get out of the rain any more than he did. Then I heard him throw the hammer in the back of Sugar's truck, and, wiping the rain off his face with the crook of his elbow, he ran over to the porch carrying a board from the shed.

Ducking onto the porch, he reached across to a clothesline that was strung between the windows and the ceiling, grabbed a striped towel off, and pulled it around *me*. I must have looked surprised. For a minute he looked at me, and I think I was expecting something, but then he tipped the end of my nose with his finger, grinned at me and sat back on this broken-down chair, his legs stretched out. For a minute, the two of us just sat there listening to the rain on the tin roof. Then he started working again, prying these nails out of the board.

"Don't you ever stop working?" I asked.

"Don't you ever stop riding?" he said and he looked over at me and winked which gave me the funniest feeling inside.

"But *I'm* trying to do something . . ." I kind of hesitated I suppose, "I've got a deadline."

"Yeah? What?"

I sidled across the floor closer and watched him pull the nail, which was pretty bent.

"It doesn't matter."

"Ah, I know, you're going to ride off into the horizon with Matt and Laurie."

"Steffie's been talking!"

"No, not Steffie. I'm not blind, Erin."

"While *you* ride off into the horizon with Bridie."

"Oh," he kind of hummed and went on nailing. "And does that bother you?"

"Not hardly." I stood up and went to the edge of the porch where I could sit without getting wet.

"You really don't like her, do you?"

"Maybe I know her better than you."

"Maybe people are different people depending on who they're with."

"You a philosopher, John Mullin?"

"You said you liked mature people." He grinned.

A stream of water was running down the unpainted porch beam, pooling on the tilting floor and I moved over so I wouldn't get wet.

"We're always fighting," I said.

"Not really," he looked back at me.

"See," I laughed.

"Why don't you come to the fair with us, Erin? We're going to the midway today and the Demolition Derby tomorrow."

I looked up at him and thought of Steffie saying the four wanted to be alone, whatever that meant, and I felt the mist falling on my left arm. "I don't think so."

"Because of the kids, right?" he said.

I nodded. "Maybe."

"Me too, Erin?"

"I don't know . . . you're different."

"Odd? Strange?"

"You sound like Steffie . . . okay, if I have to pick, you're odd. Like working hours on this silly fence and shed."

"Spending money for . . ."

"For?" I added.

"Just something."

"You really sound mysterious, you know."

"I am mysterious."

"No, you're not."

"But I am odd."

I got up and sat on the first porch step, stretching my legs out into the misty rain. "A little, but I like odd . . . I mean . . ."

I stopped.

"What do you like, Erin?"

"Oh, nothing." I really had no idea why I was feeling like I was feeling but I decided it had something to do with the rain.

"You know I think *your deadline* sounds more like some big dream."

"So? Maybe people need to dream something in order for it to happen."

"So, tell me about it."

I don't know why I told him, I hadn't even told Steffie the whole thing. It was probably the rain again. I sat back against the porch post, "I'd like to braid Shadow's hair and wash him till he shines, then ride him all the way down the beach."

"That's it?"

"Oh, you really want the whole thing?"

He nodded.

"Well, then I'd like to ride to town in time for the fair parade a week from Friday. I'd like to ride him, prancing right down Route 25 with all the locals chawing at the sides of the road. Staring. Old man Papoletti saying, 'You certainly are back!'"

"I guess you're riding with someone in particular in this dream?" he asked.

I just stared down at my sneaker which was sopping wet, squeegeeing my toes inside.

"Now, what's your dream?" I asked.

"It's not something I can tell you . . ."

He stretched his leg out and I thought his foot was going to touch mine, but it didn't. Then he looked at me out of the corner of his eye as if he were wondering if he could trust me. "But . . . want to see one?"

"See what?"

"A dream."

"Oh," I laughed. "When?"

"How about now," he said and; taking my hands, he pulled me up and, even though it was still misty, we started walking down Ratt without talking, as if we had an appointment.

Ten

At the highway we crossed, then jumped over a culvert into a grassy hollow which in the woods turns into the ravine. Pricker bushes like swooning arms picked at my legs and we walked right into a bank of sumach but John ducked under it as if he knew every bush. The ground was practically carpeted with poison ivy there, all speckled from the sun, and I worried about touching it until I saw him jump over a patch of it. He held out his hand for me to take a running jump, too.

We still didn't talk, really, and I couldn't imagine where we were going, but we dropped lower and lower down the side of the ravine as if we were going to find ourselves a prehistoric cave or something. But then I saw another kind of bone.

"There," John said, pointing to the thing.

On the side of the ravine, one side shored up with boards to make it stay balanced, was an old boat, about eighteen feet or so, with a big closed can of blue paint on the seat. We pulled ourselves through the thicket to it. Wooden strips like the ribs of a giant fish hugged the bottom and sides of it, and a wooden slit ran down the middle like an appendix scar. New white boards had just been hammered in, probably to replace rotting ones and patch-colored the sides like teeth. There was no sail, but I thought I saw a hole where one could go.

The bow was pushed right into the tangled brush and that was what I stared at, because I didn't know how the boat got way into the ravine like that or how it would get out.

"What do you think?" John said. The rain had stopped and he squatted down and chipped at a flaking fiber of board with the end of his hammer.

"I think . . . I think it's a boat." I sort of laughed.

"Not just a boat," he said. "A dory sloop."

I started to climb in, then stopped instinctively. "Okay to do this?" I asked.

"Sure." I could see he was really proud of his mysterious old dory sloop, however it got into the ravine. "It's old," he said. "I think it must have been buried under water for fifty or sixty years—that's why it didn't rot, maybe when the ravine was full of water.

"But how did it get way up here?"

"Storm probably, but I don't know. All I know is that it's here and it's mine."

"It couldn't have washed in around 1913, could it?" I asked, and he hadn't heard of the Big Storm and I told him and I could tell he liked the idea that maybe that was how his boat got there. Probably because there is something great about feeling you're part of something that matters like that. But I was rubbing my hands along the gunnels of the boat, rocking it lightly when he said, really proudly,

"Sturdy, huh?"

I didn't answer. I sort of whispered, hunching down,

and leaning toward the center. *"Hang on! This wind keeps swinging! It's like a tornado!"*

And he caught on just like that. "Grab the center board!" he called from the rear, crouching down against the sea.

"The sails have gone," I shouted back.

"She'll make it. Run with the wind."

I looked up at where the torn sails should have been, gripped the handle and squinted into our raging wind, and suddenly he climbed up next to me and grabbed the center board, too.

And we rode like that for a minute, right through our storm, then we caught each other's eye, and laughed as if we had caught each other at something, and laughed more.

"What do you think?" he said proudly.

"I think wrecks don't always stay wrecks. In fact, *things* don't really die."

"Just people?"

"Yeah, . . . they do, don't they." Old people . . . but my grandparents were only in their early seventies, I thought. Not old. I didn't have to worry about them dying, not now anyway.

Then I asked, "How do you think you will ever get this out of the ravine into the lake?" It was thick with white birch trees between the boat and the beach.

He shrugged his shoulders and hung his hands down between his legs, picking up a tack that had fallen into the bottom of the boat, as if he were embarrassed.

"I don't know," he looked up at me, grinning, "but I know I'll get it out."

"Stubborn," I said and realized I sounded like my own father.

"Being stubborn only helps, I figure," he said.

I stood up. Through the trees I could see patches of sun on the water, and clouds had drifted over the lake, leaving small puffs in a blue blue sky.

"Hey, thanks for showing me," I said as I stepped out.

"It's all right." He looked at me long again the way he did, then he stood up in the dory. I think he was sorry to see me go. "You're still going to the Luddys' alone?"

"Hey, I'm stubborn, too," I said. "I'm doing fine at the Luddys'," and I looked for the tiny side trail that led through the poison ivy.

"See, Erin, there's something about Luddy that always bothered me when I worked there, you know? Like, he never seems to have anything to do."

"They're poor—small farmers."

"I never saw anyone work like some of the other small farmers on Ratt Road. No, it's something else. He never seemed to like me, almost just because I was a summer kid or something, and, well . . . one day he backed his truck into the goose shed and killed three geese, feathers everywhere. He just gunned away."

"Maybe it was an accident."

"Maybe he drinks."

"Look, at least the Luddys keep their German shepherd tied up, that's what I worry about, not sleepy old Mr. Luddy sneaking up to the barn loft to sneak a few."

"Okay, okay," John said ahead of me, cutting out some of the straggling tree vines with his pocket knife as he walked. "I'm supposed to go to the fair now, so, well . . . just be careful, okay?"

I grinned at his worrying. "Look, I don't need a brother." I admit I almost wished he'd asked me one more time to go to the fair.

Eleven

It started to rain again and it rained all day and all night, so the next morning when I found Steffie was still quarantined on the porch with P.I., I didn't think twice about going on to the Luddys' alone. I had to get Shadow out to the open field. Even if it was just for a little while.

When I came to the Luddy house the yard was empty. I ran up on the porch and looked through the screen. "Mrs. Luddy," I called through the screen, which I never liked to do because I hated to have that dog growl back at me even though I knew he was locked on the other side. But there was no one there, not even the dog. I could just hear this school wall-clock ticking in the other room real slow. Tock. Tock, "Mrs. Luddy," I called out, and when she didn't answer again, I reached around inside the door and unhooked the lead rope from the wall where she had begun keeping it.

But the yard was empty too, the way some farmyards are. An old-fashioned standing white washtub leaned against a tree near some rolls of fence wire that weeds had grown around. In the middle of the yard under a huge maple tree was a skeleton of a lawn swing, no cushions, with weeds growing up through the bottom of it. A gray, rain-ruined shed with a small window lay on its side with an empty can of tar next to it, its legs pulled right out of the ground and sticking out to the side, stiff. Lawnchairs with no one in them.

I thought it looked like what I would think a field would look like after a battle and I did wonder where the dog was, but only for a minute, because yesterday's rain had cleared up and I saw Shadow out there under a small maple. I started for the barn, swinging the lead rope, feeling good under the eleven o'clock sun. The geese ignored me, just went on swarming around this patch of yard by the well as I hiked by them.

The black barn looked almost toothless with its missing slats, and its ladder coming out of the upstairs loft at an angle for no reason at all. Even when the sun was so hot it burned the field, the barn was dark inside, and when I pushed open the thick creaky door, it looked pitch-black.

I don't like to be alone, even at home, because I can feel *empty*. I can hear *empty*. Just put me in an empty room and I suddenly hear the radiator, or the boards swelling, and they turn into people sounds. Stranger sounds. And a lot of times it's in my head, but the minute I stepped through that barn door I felt as if I were not alone. In the corner I could see the sun streaming in a window without glass and pouring on the saddle and bridle. I started walking across the room toward them when I heard a rustling noise, and I looked through the cracked doorway into the big empty barn and saw Mr. Luddy lying in some hay piled into a corner with empty beer bottles all around him. He was not up in the loft; he was down where the dairy cows used to be and he looked like a thick brown bull lying all fat and bony in a field, except he was wearing a yellow plaid shirt that spread where his big hairy stomach rolled out around his waist.

I stopped where I was, and I thought that I should get out of that barn. I don't even know why I thought that, Mr. Luddy never did anything to me, but I did think that. But when I turned to get out, he rolled over on his side and said, "Girl," in this throaty voice like a frog belching and I was not surprised he called me that because I never did think he knew my name.

"Hello, Mr. Luddy," I said, and I changed my plan since he had seen me. I decided to go ahead and get the saddle and bridle as if everything were just fine.

"Ain't you a summer kid?"

"Yes, sir, I am," I answered and I started walking, brisk-like, toward the saddle when I heard the straw rustling in that other room, and I decided that I was going to go right on as if I weren't worrying about anything. And I hiked the saddle up, first on my knee, then up to my waist, and I started backing out, when I saw Mr. Luddy getting up, like that old bull, first one leg, then the other, real slow, groaning something about "borrowing old Shadow, damn it," with a bottle in his hand.

But then he didn't move so slow, because before I could get to the outside door I heard the door creak between the open barn and the little room, and I saw his hand reach around the door and then I saw him standing there, his shirt stretching around these big thick shoulders, and big mud boots with broken laces, grinning at me, and his face had a beard from not shaving, but his bulging eyes looked almost bright.

And without thinking at all, I just dropped the saddle and bridle and I backed up toward the door without turning around. "Mr. Luddy?" I said. But he moved like lightning then, his thick boots crunching the straw as he went for that door behind me. Without turning around, I backed into the center of the room toward the other door, and I could hear this deep laugh gurgle in his throat—his mouth didn't even move.

I put my hand off to the side to touch the door, but when I got my fingers around the old rusty pinch handle, I felt his hairy hand around my hand, and I could feel beer breath warm on my face as he said somewhere near my cheek, "Girl," and he was grinning, but every time he opened his mouth the smell of beer squeezed out between his thick lips.

I tried to pull away, but his hand was like a steel clamp on mine, only wet and warm, and I took my other hand and grabbed the side of the door, and tried to pull myself around it into the stable as if I were climbing a rope. Only he just laughed as if it were funny that I would try to get away. He laughed, and said, "Summer girl," with this beer breath even though his lips didn't move, and my thoughts were getting mixed up I was so scared, and as I tried to pull myself, just around the corner, I heard far off,

"Leon!" Mrs. Luddy was home and calling him. "Leon," she was calling him, and I could feel a weakening in his hand, and that second, I pulled myself loose and flung myself around the door and through the crack into the stable. He stomped across the hay after me through this big room, sort of breathing hard like an animal breathes through his lips.

"Leon," I heard again, and the voice was closer, but I had made the opposite wall, both hands flat against it, and I pulled the huge sliding door aside and squeezed out a narrow slit, too narrow for the bull behind me. Then I started walking across the barnyard, in big lanky steps like my Aunt Shirley used to take, when Mrs. Luddy came up to the fence and leaned over, pushing curls of hair back into the braid at her neck.

"You riding, Erin?" she asked me, her cheeks shiny and round, the fence nearly to her chin. She had the dog at her side on a leash.

"Ah, yeah," I said and I tried not to breathe hard because I didn't want her to know her husband was hiding in the barn, watching me probably, because the barn hadn't been just *empty,* there had been someone there. "I'm just going to ride now," I said, and I walked over to Shadow, who was tearing the dry weeds out from around the pole, and he swung his head over once and nudged my arm with the back of his nose.

"What about a saddle?" Mrs. Luddy said, but she didn't know *he* was in there by the saddle smelling like that and that I wasn't going back in there. "And the bridle?"

"I'm . . . riding bareback today," I said, quick. Then I put my fingers through the halter ring and led Shadow over to the fence, and I climbed up the slats of the fence as if they were a ladder, and that horse didn't even move as I threw my leg over him, and slid onto his warm, sleek back.

"Ooooh, boy," I said. And I grabbed on to his mane and slowly steered him into the main part of the barnyard when I saw John riding that bike of his up the lane beside the Luddy house. Mrs. Luddy leaned over the bleached rail fence and she smiled as I pulled Shadow around by his mane and nudged him in the ribs with my legs.

When John dropped his bike and came up next to her at the fence, she said without turning her head, "Isn't this girl something?"

And I wondered why John had come over when he had planned to go to the fair, but I thought I knew, in fact I knew all right. But I had been right too, I didn't need him.

Twelve

I didn't know what to do. I kept smelling beer breath and remembering and I didn't ever want to go back to that barn again, but I had to get Shadow out into the open field if I ever wanted to be with Laurie and Matt. It was too late to get another horse. I thought if Steffie went with me, Luddy wouldn't dare hide around, and once I got out of the fenced yard, he wouldn't be able to catch me and Shadow anyway. Then I worried about leaving Steffie behind by the barn when I went out riding, and I was lying in my bed the next morning worrying that way when I heard a shotgun go off.

Sometimes when I tell kids at home about my grandfather, they don't believe me, and I don't blame them. I ran downstairs without even looking out the window, and from the porch I saw a little puff of smoke floating up from the pumphouse, and I thought, I'm going to see blood all over the beach, but I didn't. I saw my grandfather standing in front of the pumphouse, his shotgun resting in his arm. He was wearing a ski mask.

Without telling him I had seen him, I ran back in the

house and through the kitchen and then into the bathroom. "Grandma," I shouted, "Grandma!" But she was nowhere, and I wondered if my grandfather had caught Matt riding across the beach, or worse, in the pumphouse, and I knew that even though there might be blood on the beach I had to go down there.

When I got to the beach, though, my grandfather was creeping closer and closer to the pumphouse, squinting through his woolly ski mask.

"Stand back," he said, and I saw that he wasn't aiming at a motorcycle, he was aiming up at the roof where there was a yellow jacket nest and some yellow jackets already swarming like little bits of black paper, and before I could say anything at all to him, he fired again. This time he hit the whole side of the roof, and the yellow jackets exploded like a Mexican piñata that someone had smashed open. Buzzing everywhere.

"Now I got them," he yelled out, but the blast had jarred his glasses off, and, discovering it, he dropped to the ground and started groping around in the weeds mumbling, "Damn, my new plastic ones!" And the yellow jackets were spreading out farther and farther, little black and yellow spots everywhere, and I saw one land on his arm and another on his neck, and there were some swarming around his pants.

"Grandpa," I shouted at him, but it was too late. Before he could get away, six yellow jackets stung him and each bite puffed up on his skin the size of a raspberry.

But he wasn't done. I was still deciding whether to go to the Luddys' with Steffie or not when my grandfather took gasoline down to where the nest blew off and lit the torn nest with fire, so that suddenly I saw flames shooting up, almost licking the birch tree. I knew my grandma could handle this, but she wasn't anywhere, so when my grandfather climbed up the stairs—his face all sooty—I tried to talk to him, but he was still mad at me, so he didn't talk. He had to put the vinegar on the bites alone (he spilled it all over the sink), and I decided I was going to Luddys' whether it was risky or not.

I was not even going to think about Mr. Luddy, and I was not going to tell anyone about him either because then no one would let me ride Shadow. As for Steffie, she could walk out in the fields with me while I rode.

Steffie had been lying on her back for three days, scratching, and when I met her at the highway, she had all sorts of information that she was going to give me if I wanted it or not. She began with Matt's motorcycle.

"He doesn't just ride the motorcycle on the beach. Sometimes he hides it there. I saw it in Tracy's ravine when I went for a walk with my mother to show her where I got in poison ivy."

"So?"

"He wasn't with it."

"So?"

"I wonder what he does when he's not with his cycle."

"Oh, Steffie."

"Maybe he breaks into pumphouses."

"I'm sure."

"And boat houses."

"He's no criminal, Steffie."

"Well, everyone is worried, Erin, because everything that's happening lately is happening closer and closer and you know about last night and . . ."

"What happened last night?"

"*Someone* got into Jackman's boat house and broke the cables and machine that lower the boat into the lake. And Mrs. Everson's cottage. Whoever it was even broke windows," she began, and even though I wondered why my grandfather missed that piece of news, for the first time I thought to myself it sounds like more than one person is breaking in. But I didn't tell her that. I just looked bored, so she changed the subject.

"John went with the kids to the fair last night," she began after a few seconds, and I already knew because John had told me but now I wondered if that was where they went for sure.

"And they went to the Demolition Derby," Steffie said, "and they bet on real crashers, and John bet on a Number 46 Ford painted with red and purple lightning and it bashed all the other cars even though it didn't even have a hood. He won two dollars in bets and he bought Bridie a silver chain," she ended, and I felt something turn over in the middle of me.

"Do you care?' she said, sort of impishly.

"No, I don't care."

"Maybe you do," she said, lifting her chin up at me.

"Think it," I said. There are just so many things a person can worry about, and when we got to Sugar's and I didn't see John fixing fences or sheds, I knew he had gone off to the fair again or to the Olmstead House or somewhere with Bridie Kelly, and I didn't even care. Really.

Sometimes I thought Mrs. Luddy just liked being with Steffie and me, but that day I guessed she must have figured something out about yesterday, because she came out the minute we passed the door and she trailed us all the way to the barn, wiping her wisps of hair behind her ears. She had no dog with her. The sun made her forehead look shiny and she had a kind of lipless grin.

"Going after him again?" she said, sort of nervously, and the geese let her walk right through them, parting like · the Red Sea when she swept by in her long print housedress. Steffie skipped along just behind her, taking advantage of the safe path she made. If Mrs. Luddy really knew about yesterday, she didn't let on.

I kept watching the windows in the barn and then the opening in the loft. Maybe I would always watch every window in every barn, but I didn't see any face, and I was glad Mrs. Luddy had come.

When I finished saddling Shadow, I poked his belly so he'd let out the air that he had stored to stop me from fastening the girth strap. I knew I was partly excited and partly scared—I could feel it there right below my ribs—and I scratched Shadow's neck before getting on, just stalling. Then, I looked across the fence toward the highway at the cars whizzing by in gray blurs. Stalling some more. Finally, I climbed on Shadow and rode around the barnyard but he kept kicking out at flies that landed on his rump and on his side. I just hung on, hoping he wasn't going to buck me off.

After a few rides around the yard, though, I shouted, "He's too crazy today," and I started to climb off when I looked over the fence and saw two horses cantering down the outside field toward us.

Against the sun, all I could see were shadows, but my heart pounded in my throat because I just knew one of the riders was Laurie.

Not until they cantered into the near field, did I know I was wrong. Looking like Don Quixote and his partner or something, a tall girl was riding toward us on a big red horse with a boy on a fat gray pony, his legs sticking out like popsicle sticks, wobbling across the field behind her. It was Sugar . . . *and John.*

Thirteen

"How about a ride?" Sugar called across the field. Dressed in neat English jodhpurs instead of her usual Levi's, and a man's white shirt, she looked as if she were ready to go jumping in a horse show or something. I couldn't believe they'd come.

"Say yes, Erin," Steffie whispered, and climbed up on a post.

"You're coming, too, Steffie," Sugar said, pulling Missy up along the outside of the fence.

"Come on in," I yelled.

"No, no, Erin." Sugar laughed, and she pointed to the outside field. "Out here!"

I was trapped. But as we started out the gate and into the field at a walk, I thought, it can't last long. That helped, and I forgot about everything else.

Riding out that day we were something to see. Steffie, her legs practically in splits, straddling Missy behind Sugar in her fancy jodhpurs, John on a pony half his size, me on big Shadow, King of the Weeds.

None of us exactly fit.

I looked across the field, where not only could I see the highway, I could see the lake as if someone had water-colored it right up over the trees. Shadow's head pulled down with each step as he hustled to corner second spot in the single file of horses. My hands were cold and sweaty but when he reached down to steal the tassle of a weed, I pulled his head up.

"Cut it out, Horse!" I said.

"You getting tough?" John called out from the pony.

"I've always been tough," I told him, and I thought about the silver chain even though I had decided not to and even though John hadn't gone to the fair today, but I said, "I thought you didn't ride."

"I don't," he said, and grinned up at me and it reminded me of when we were sitting on the porch arguing.

"Well, you look pretty silly on that pony."

"So if the car runs, I'll buy it," he said. "You should see me pick a wreck!"

"I heard," I said, and I kneed Shadow to move ahead.

"What did you hear?" he called out as I went.

"Enough," I said but I was too far ahead for him to ask me what enough was.

There wasn't much talking as we headed across the flat field toward the border of trees and I felt my hands grow warmer. Even Steffie seemed happy just straddling there behind Sugar not talking, her toes bouncing out at each of the horses' steps. Before we reached the woods, we rode through a dotty field of black-eyed Susans, their eyes bobbing on long stems. A single deer at the edge of the woods stood and just stared at us, then broke sideways, and leapt across the field, its tail flagging like a fluffy white rag.

Seeing the deer, Shadow stopped, but didn't bolt, and I just hung on, praying. I really didn't want to be run with.

Funny, though, as we rode, ducking low, leafy trees

through the woods, not talking, something happened between the four of us. I could feel it. The smell of pine needles was all around me and the hooves fell soft on the path. Leafless lower branches looked like arms and fingers stretched out, and slowly, I knew what was happening. We were standing up to something by riding across the fenceless field, past the deer, the pond, and it had sort of connected us.

All of a sudden I knew that we should go back still feeling this way, before something went wrong, when Sugar said, "Okay, you guys, let's go for a little run."

She never gave me a chance to say "No!" At a spot that breaks into a narrow green pasture, Sugar started trotting Missy, then she broke her into a canter.

The pony ran next, passing me to catch up with Missy. At first I held tight, my hands frozen. But when I caught sight of the round rump of the pony cantering past me like milk-white motion or something, John's legs bobbing up and down at either side, I started loosening the rein on Shadow.

"Whoopee," Steffie shouted ahead, her pigtails bouncing.

"Go!" John shouted as he bent over the pony's mane.

I felt myself getting caught up in their heat and I suddenly let the rein loose between my fingers, and Shadow started to run, his tall, giant legs reaching out for the pasture in front of us.

"Hey!" John grinned across at me as we caught up with the pony.

I smiled back though I already knew *I couldn't slow Shadow.*

"Way to go, Erin!" Steffie yelled. I was out of control and I knew if Shadow could find a shortcut, he'd take off toward the highway.

Then I started to feel what was happening under me, and I realized *Shadow wasn't running crazy*, he was just running, cantering side by side Missy, the two horses, their necks all stretched out, puffing sort of quiet as they ran. Sugar, her hair flying out in back of her, smiled around her shoulder.

I felt wonderful. The three horses were flying down the narrow pasture path, this soft thudding of their hooves under us in perfect rhythm when I caught sight of a fallen tree trunk lying across the path. I panicked. But at the log—miracle!—the horses just glided over, one by one, landing like music on the other side, and running ahead. Shadow too.

I leaned over him, my chin nearly touching his mane, and I loved that big horse right then. "Good boy," I whispered, and rubbed his warm neck as we ran.

At the end of the narrow corridor, the path turns right, and Sugar pulled Missy up to a trot, then a walk, and Shadow slowed down to a walk, following Missy automatically, with no fuss at all.

A huge crow dived down across the opening in the woods, its black wings shiny in the sunlight. The air began to feel hot and heavy and the sweat of the horse stung my nose sweetly, a new smell to me.

"Man, wait a minute," John said, laughing. He and his wobbly pony were trying to catch up to Shadow, the King, two trots to every one of Shadow's.

"That pony's about the same size as that silly bike," I shouted.

"It's getting me where I want to go." He looked up at me, teasing, his skin peeling along the crack of his nose, just like Steffie's.

"Where do you want to go?" I heard myself playing, forgetting about the silver chain.

"Someplace with you," he said, and I was not going to look at him, but I did and I felt the wind on my cheeks, because they were warm.

"I'll walk home with you, Erin, if you'll walk back to Sugar's with me while I put the pony away," he said.

I waited for a minute but then I said, "Sounds okay." Still warm. I had beaten the open field, I had beaten Shadow and I liked the way John was making me feel.

"Maybe we'll stop by the boat," he shouted as he kneed the pony again and went flying along the edge of the weeds, passing me and Shadow and catching up with Missy.

"Yes!" I shouted back.

I couldn't believe what I was seeing when we rode back across the field to the Luddys' barnyard. *Laurie was straddling the fence.* My heart started to go crazy just seeing her.

"Laurie!" I shouted.

"Hey, Montana!" she smiled back and waved at me. She was wearing her white cowboy hat with the blue feather. "I came to see that horse," she said. "Can he outrace the Barts?"

"He can," I said, and I forgot Sugar and John were still there. I laughed. "He could run scout for a thousand wild ponies," I said, and I forgot Steffie.

"All of them white?" she played.

"Yes," and I reined Shadow into the yard and pulled the gate shut with the rope that hung on the side, leaving the others outside.

"I'll go home with Sugar," Steffie said to me from behind Sugar's back, and I said, "Okay, Steffie, good idea," and I forgot that I had said I'd walk home with John and that maybe we'd stop by the boat. When I remembered and looked at him, he was pulling the pony angrily around, and he started trotting back across the field. All I could see was his back.

"John!" I called. He didn't answer, but I couldn't worry now. "Where's Matt?" I said to Laurie.

"I don't know," she said. "Say, is that big fleabag ready for the beach?" She laughed and stuck the heels of her boots between the fence slats.

"Is he ready!" I said, and I looked up at the sky, "I think so," and I folded my shoulders a little, shyly I suppose. I just kept looking at her, there. I could hardly believe she was in the Luddys' yard.

"I'll walk home with you, Erin," she said as I slid off Shadow without climbing down the fence and started unhooking the girth, and I looked back at her and I smiled at her and I slid the saddle off, the metal piece slapping against my leg.

"Need help?" she asked, her long hair blowing from the east wind coming off the lake across the field.

"Nope," I said, and I hiked the saddle up and started for the little room. I didn't care if Mr. Luddy was in there or not because Laurie was here.

Fourteen

Laurie and I walked down Ratt Road as if there were nobody there but us and I could tell she was mad at Matt because she said sometimes he rode off on his motorcycle alone and didn't tell her where he was going or what he was doing and she was left alone. I could tell she didn't like it, too, even though she was saying that she really didn't mind because he needed to be with his friends. And I wondered if that was where he was. And I knew she had come to find me because he was gone but I didn't care, I was just so glad to be walking with Laurie Kelly down Ratt Road.

We talked about everything. I asked her if she remembered the time we were afraid of the katydid and taped a Dixie cup over it on the window, and she told me Grandma Kelly missed the two of us always gossiping in her rocking chairs late at night. And before we split at the Y in the road, this time we picked a real date to meet each other on our horses because I thought, I am almost ready, and we picked Friday.

"I'll call you tomorrow," Laurie said, "to see how you're doing."

And when I went to bed that night, I couldn't sleep. I heard the waves exploding into the bluff, and I knew the water was hissing around the rocks by the pumphouse, and I thought of a hundred things—getting a hose out to the barnyard to wash Shadow, finding some metal polish for his stirrups—but I didn't sleep.

When I got up in the morning and saw my grandfather sitting at the kitchen table with his shotgun pointed out the window, I didn't even think anything about it. I knew he shot at crows that landed on his corn stalks every summer, but I knew he didn't really aim at them. One time he shot and split the top of a corn stalk and a crow just flew away. But I didn't talk to him either, because the war was still going on, and I was not going to give in. If he didn't want to talk to me forever, fine.

My grandmother came up and scratched my back as I was eating my cereal.

"How is my perfect child?" she whispered, then she pinched me and winked to let me know she didn't really think I was so perfect. She has a lot of patience when it comes to the kind of wars my grandfather gets into. She pitches in to fight the ones she can, and she stays out of others. She was staying out of our war. Maybe because I figured all that out, I told her what I had been doing mornings. And I told her,

"I'm going to ride Shadow out into the field today alone." I whispered because I still didn't want my grandfather to know.

"Alone?" she said.

"Alone," I said.

"You are something, Erin, training that horse by yourself and riding it all over. I never would tackle that kind of challenge, not me." Then she pulled out the extension ladder and picked it up and set it against the roof. "Be careful, baby," she said.

I guess you have to understand where the pumphouse sat in order to understand what happened next. It sat about twenty feet from where a ravine used to be, but where there wasn't one now because someone filled it up with dirt and people used it as a trail to get to the beach. When my grandfather put the fence up, he figured that a motorcycle would have a big problem getting to the beach without that path so he drove the fence spikes halfway into the trail. Anything or anyone would have to go off the trail and up the bank to get past the fence to the beach.

Building the fence that way must have been like waving a red handkerchief in front of Matt Calley, because I had not left for the barn that day when I heard this clanking sound, and when I looked down the bluff, Matt had a sledgehammer and was whacking the metal fence spikes with it, bending them in half. His hair was curly all over his head and wet from the waves that were still splashing around the rocks and through the fence.

At first my grandfather didn't hear the noise, but not much escaped his ears, and when he heard the hammering he ran out to the bluff.

My grandmother ran out after him, and put her hand through my grandfather's arm as if that would help, but it didn't this time, because the minute my grandfather saw Matt Calley with that sledgehammer, he exploded. His eyes flashing, he ran back into the kitchen and picked up the gun, but, thank goodness, he stopped and, setting the gun behind the rocker, he started out for the stairs with nothing in his hands at all.

"Now, Thomas," my grandmother said as we kept right behind him, but he didn't even seem to hear her. His cigar solid in his teeth, his dark eyes were blazing. At the landing, he put his fingers on his lips, and gave us a look that said *do not follow me* and he turned and walked quietly down the stairs. I felt as if I were looking at a time bomb. At the second landing, he swung under the railing, right into the brush, and, squatting down, tunneled through the bramble on the bluff that backed the pumphouse.

Near the fence, he pulled himself into a tunnel of what I thought were grapevines though I have never seen any grapes on them, but I have hidden in them. And when Matt headed for the spike at the back of the pumphouse, two feet from where Grandpa was hiding, Grandpa jumped out at him, his fingers spread like claws or something.

Matt just laughed, and he backed up and pulled his hands away as if he refused to touch Grandpa, but this made Grandpa furious so he pulled his fist back and punched at him. That was when Matt spinned away, cut through the brush, and started running down the beach. But my grandfather didn't just stand in the bushes or something, he ran after him.

"My God, he thinks he's twenty-one," my grandmother said, hustling down the stairs, but she wasn't laughing, she was pale.

Barefoot, Matt ran down the beach like a black wind, but my grandfather was not two feet behind him, his arms moving like pistons, his knees high, running and running. The two of them, like the wind. They ran down past the curve in the beach and they ran past the jetty, scrambling over it as if it were a wall in a Marine obstacle course, and they ran past the Tracys' steps.

I couldn't believe my grandfather. He hadn't lost an inch, and his arms were shiny from sweat, but, his legs quick, he ran like a little machine, and I thought, I will never forget this.

But then my grandpa jumped off the next jetty and caught Matt's shirt, and when Matt turned, my grandfather threw a punch at him that caught him in the neck and Matt fell down in the sand. My grandmother and I started running again to try and stop them. But red-faced, the veins in his neck all sticking out, Matt got to his feet and, like some bear, picked my grandfather up around the chest and squeezed. I saw my grandpa crumble. And Matt walked him out into the water and simply threw him out into the waves as if he were something he could throw away. An old plastic milk carton or something.

I started running toward him alongside my grandmother, but then I saw my grandfather get up slowly from the water, dripping wet, and start back into shore, and now I could see he was a seventy-year-old man and I forgave everything. As far as I was concerned the war between us was over.

Matt had run ahead of us and, as we walked back, I saw him cut up the ravine toward the Kelly house and I wondered what Laurie would say when she saw his neck all red and I thought, she'll understand, she'll know Grandpa is old and she'll know the fight had nothing to do with me.

But by the time I spent the morning waiting for the phone to ring again and Laurie didn't call, I knew that my grandfather had done it again. He might be a seventy-year-old man but it was hard being on his side. When he came downstairs in dry clothes, and my grandmother handed him a corned beef sandwich as he lay on the couch, and he grumbled, "I hate corned beef on white" (he looked tired—I remember that now), I didn't say anything back. He might be like a little boy but didn't even little boys have to grow up?

Fifteen

In the afternoon Steffie and Mrs. Luddy walked me to the barnyard again, and if Mr. Luddy was there I didn't see him. I rode for a half hour or so in there, but after that I pulled the rope on the gate and went outside alone, and for the first time I began to feel comfortable out in the field even though there were no fences, not as if Shadow were going to run to the highway with me.

I didn't just walk him either. I cantered him straight across the field, then past the pond, I trotted him, then I turned him into the orchard and raced him between the trees. "Okay, King," I whispered, "Go!" He flew.

I was cooling him down when I saw four specks coming down Ratt Road, and I realized that it was Bridie and Danny Kelly and Mary and John.

For a minute I thought I would duck back into the orchard with Shadow and I felt the reins sweaty in my hands, but the specks started waving and I realized they had seen me. I pulled Shadow slow over to the side of the road and walked toward them. The Olmstead House is at the end of Ratt Road and I guessed they were coming back from playing cards or whatever it was they did there. It was too early for the fair.

"Hey," Danny called out. "You finally coming over to the Olmstead House, Olive Oyl?"

"Not with that animal!" Mary said. She and Danny were holding hands, two and two.

John and Bridie were behind them.

"Steffie wouldn't like that," Bridie laughed. John didn't say anything.

I hadn't seen him since the day Laurie and I walked home together after our ride with Sugar and I hadn't talked to Bridie since the bonfire, but I thought I'll have to talk to her—and him—someday and I figured that talking to them from the top of Shadow couldn't be all bad. They were into being pairs, so, Shadow and I were a pair. A car went by and didn't slow down, and the dust curled up into Shadow's face, and I felt him get nervous, but I held my legs firm and kept moving toward them.

I guess what I am saying is I was ready at least to make friends, you know, getting myself psyched, when all of a sudden Bridie flicked her cigarette away, grabbed this red-striped beach towel out of John's hands and started running toward me, flicking it out, as if Shadow were a bull.

"Come on, Ferdinand!" she shouted, laughing, and I could feel Shadow's back arch under me, and I whispered, "Easy, boy."

John said, "Knock it off, Bridie." But she flicked the towel at him, too, and kept coming at Shadow.

"I want to see how the big rider from Connecticut can ride." She grinned back at Mary and sort of squatted and flicked the towel again, and Shadow pulled his nose back as if he weren't sure what he would do, and I tried to steady him. But all of a sudden Bridie let out this "Whoooppee" as if she were in a rodeo or something and ran at him, and Shadow sat back on his heels, turned, almost throwing me off, then began to run.

It all happened too fast. I leaned over him, my chin practically touching his mane, but Shadow was running past a canter, past a gallop, something wild and scared, and he didn't care where he was running. He headed right back into Papoletti's orchard. But it's an old orchard, the crookedy limbs of the trees cocked at all different angles like elbows and when one cocked down in front of him suddenly, Shadow dodged it. And the limb cut across the saddle and into my stomach, sweeping me right off his back into the air. Shadow raced on without me between the row of trees.

I landed hard, lying in high weeds with something hard stinging my face. Then I reached up and pulled my fingers gently across my cheek. I looked at them. Something had scratched me—I didn't even know what—I was bleeding. I hadn't moved when I heard someone come up behind me.

"Erin," I heard John's voice and someone else was with him. I saw Danny's boots.

"Are you all right?" John asked.

"Leave me alone," I said.

He bent over to take my arm, but I could feel myself growing embarrassed and mad and sore. "Just leave me alone," and I guess I wanted him to say he wouldn't leave me alone. I guess I wanted him to lean over and help me sit up and put his arm around my shoulders and wonder if something were broken even though I told him not to, but he didn't. The second time I said "Go away," I could feel his feet pause near my arm, then he turned and crunched away through the orchard and Danny followed him.

And lying there I thought, I don't belong with my grandma and grandpa, I don't belong with Steffie or Sugar or these kids . . . or Laurie, I don't belong anywhere.

Sixteen

I chased Shadow around the orchard for thirty minutes before he let me get near him. Then I finally walked him back to the Luddys' barn. It was late, and the cottage was empty when I got back. I could see that through the windows as I let myself in through the back door.

"Grandma!" I shouted. I didn't like the empty house. "Grandma!"

I ran upstairs and found all the beds made, my grandmother's perfume bottles all arranged in neat rows, the vacuum's wire and plug all wound perfectly and the vacuum tucked into a corner. Downstairs the Blue Willow plates had been wiped dry and set back in their stacks in the dining room cupboard.

When I caught sight of an envelope taped to the front screen, I ripped it off, for some reason feeling both better that I had found it, and scared.

"Taking Grandpa into Port Huron, don't worry. Be back by five for dinner. Put on the oven for a casserole I have in the refrigerator. (Grandpa says, listen for the pumphouse bell.)" I kept rereading the envelope. Why would she take Grandpa to Port Huron without telling me in the morning? And why was she saying, don't worry? I don't worry, unless someone says don't worry.

I stood up and pressed my face against a pane in the back door glass and looked down the curving driveway toward the highway. Then I realized that both the dentist and the doctor were in Port Huron and for the first time I remembered how tired my Grandpa looked after the fight.

Walking back to the front door, I looked out across the empty apron of grass and beyond it at a freighter moving slow across the lake. Then I took another look. The ship had a double cabin and huge freight cranes and what seemed to be radar scanners, though it was hard to tell for sure from there. Even so, I was pretty certain *it was the tanker* Cort. After all my grandfather's watching, I was seeing the *Cort.* I knew his binoculars would catch every wire, but as I looked quickly around the room I realized I didn't even know where he kept them hidden.

Sort of lonesome, I sat back in my grandpa's orange chair, the smell of his cigars all around me. Cigar smells weren't so bad, not if you got used to them, I thought, and I ran my finger across a spot in the arm of the chair where my grandfather sat after he had been greasing one of his machines and before my grandma could catch him and talk him into a tub. I would tell him about the *Cort* the minute he walked in, I thought.

I had no idea how much time had passed when Steffie came to the back door and begged me to go swimming at Whale Rock with her. She had been wanting to go at night, she said.

"You sure you won't come?" Steffie asked.

"I'm sure," I said from the chair.

"Please," she begged.

"No, Steffie."

"You mad at me, Erin?" she asked, her nose against the screen again.

"No, Steffie."

"I liked riding," she said.

"Good."

"But I wouldn't want to ride with Bridie and Mary and those kids."

"They don't have horses, Steffie."

"I like to ride with you, Erin, and Sugar and John."

"What?" I tried to laugh. "You like to ride with your own brother?"

She pulled her head down almost shyly, "He's not like just any brother," she said, and neither of us talked for a minute.

"He's strange, right?" I smiled at her and she mugged, her lower lip stuck out like an Olympic boxer or something, and I said, "We'll go riding again, Steffie. I promise. The two of us will go again."

"Maybe I'll be Wichita." Now she grinned.

"Okay, okay, Wichita."

"Tomorrow?"

"Maybe tomorrow," I more or less promised, and she whooped and galloped away, slapping her rump as she ducked under the willow between our cottages.

But I didn't move and I was almost sorry she was gone as it started to get darker and darker outside. Sometimes she wasn't so bad, I decided, even if she was just a runt.

But then my head got busy. I imagined that the run after Matt must have hurt Grandpa. Maybe his heart. Maybe all that hauling of rocks didn't help. Maybe like Grandma Kelly he'd have to sit in a chair and be able to walk only if he had a Henry-walker to lean on. I felt my mouth growing dry even though nothing had really happened. I just couldn't imagine someone like the Captain not being able

111

to clean his spark plugs, or throw rocks around a pumphouse, or defend his cottage-ship against a storm. Or run.

Most of all I was sorry we had fought, and I said to myself, what if I never see him again?

But at eight o'clock I heard the car sputter up the driveway, then the door slam, voices coming into the rear of the house, and Grandpa finally exploded into the doorway.

"Just leave me alone, I'm going out on the porch!"

"Thomas, they told you to take it easy!"

He snapped around at Grandma who was being her plump robin self again, scurrying around after him with his jacket in her hands.

"*They?* You mean those weasley little women in their white caps stabbing you with those needles they carry around?"

My grandma looked over at me and up at the ceiling and I realized my grandpa had found another war. "He wouldn't even let the doctor finish the examination," she whispered to me. "Said he didn't like the smells in the examining room."

I was just so glad that he was okay! I pushed myself out of the chair so he could sit down, and my grandma tried to lead him there by the arm.

"I'm not sitting! I'm not an invalid! And I am not ready to pop off!" he said, then muttered to himself, "Those damn weasley little nurses with their needles."

He said something under his breath about who knew what was in those needles as he went out the doorway onto the porch, grabbing his binoculars from behind the curtain as he went.

"See anything?" he shouted to me. It had been a long time since he had shouted anything to me.

"A tanker," I said, "I think it was the *Cort.*"

"The *Cort!*" he bellowed. "Now, see what I missed, damn it. I haven't seen the *Cort* in two months. Probably hauling parts. It's your fault, Ethel, that's the last time I listen to you." He pushed his glasses up the bridge of his nose and peered into his binoculars through the screen. The sky was already growing a deeper blue and I saw an ocean freighter out on the lake, lights all along its long sleek iron body.

My grandma sat down, looking tired, took the straps of her purse off her arm one at a time, and I came over to the couch and sat next to her. I rubbed her back, thinking I didn't remember her back being so small and round.

"What's wrong with Grandpa?" I whispered.

"He's got a hernia, probably from moving all those rocks. Or running."

"A what?" I asked.

"A *hernia,*" she whispered, but he bellowed again from the porch.

"Ethel!" he threatened. "I don't want to hear that word." And he set the binoculars back in their case and without even shutting it climbed up the stairs by twos.

I waited until I heard the bedroom door close. "Why doesn't he want you to say 'hernia'?" I asked, ducking my head as if maybe the ceiling would come down if Grandpa heard me.

"Because the doctor said it was a weakness in the . . . *intestines,* dear," she whispered, "and he's embarrassed enough that anything could be wrong with him, and most of all that it has to be a *hernia.*" And I thought she was laughing as she always did when my grandpa did some- thing outrageous, but then I saw that even though she was laughing, her eyes were wet around the rims. They looked young and scared as if she were a little girl and something was happening that she couldn't do anything about.

And I was thinking about my grandma's eyes when I saw a fist knocking at the back door and I looked through the glass and saw Patrolman Anders.

"The Captain here?" he asked before we even opened the door.

My grandma shook her head no, and opening the door said, "He's gone upstairs for the night."

"Well, there's been more," he said, and I backed up to the arm of the couch and sat down because I wanted to hear and I didn't want to hear.

"Come in, Jim," my grandma said, glancing up the stairs as she said it. "Want a cup of coffee?"

He shook his head no. "Have you seen anything—*anything*—unusual around here?"

"No," she said. "But then we haven't been here . . . still, the bell hasn't been ringing, has it, Erin? And we haven't seen tracks, and well, no, I guess we haven't seen anything."

"Well, whoever it is got into Ruckheyser's new car, you know, that four-wheel drive he just bought, and slashed the upholstery, then as if he were in some hurry, sprang the door. Stains all over. Just keep your doors locked. Car doors, too. Might want to put your lawn mower in the shed for the night, you know, just to be safe, though he's probably done tearing the place up tonight." He shook his head and, taking his cap off for a minute, brushed his hair back with his fingers, then he said good night, and went out.

114

Seventeen

The heat that poured into my room that night wasn't a good heat. It was heavy and moved slowly by pushing its way like thick smoke through the window screens and falling on me like a hand pressing down. I could hardly breathe.

Nighttime used to be when I became Montana. I'd lie on my back and think up a patch of desert, some place where there were huge red rocks like fingers sticking up, and even though I knew the Barts were there somewhere, I'd ride my White in, never afraid of seeing the Barts ride out at us. I'd just keep my hand on my gun and start firing, and if the shoot-out got too tough, I'd roll over and think about something else. Once, I crawled out of bed and turned on the lights for a half hour or so the way I used to when I was a little kid.

But this wasn't like that. This was real, and real was hard. Like, I knew that Laurie and Matt were usually at Sugar's farm afternoons, and I wanted to ride Shadow to Sugar's to surprise Laurie and Matt there. I wanted to see the expression on their faces when they saw the King, his tail all braided, and his peppered coat shining because I brushed it so hard.

But I couldn't stop thinking that even if Matt didn't rip anyone's car, he threw my grandfather in the water like an old milk carton, and even though I knew my grandfather built a fence across his path, my grandfather was the Captain. And I wondered if seventy years didn't earn a person something. Sure, it earns him his own ship, I said to myself. A place of his own. And it earns him respect, I said to myself.

But then I also said, Matt is a person, too, and he may not like getting punched in the neck, captain or not, and I was arguing with myself that way when I thought of Laurie with the sun on her hair, sitting on the fence when I rode in from the field, smiling at me. And I thought of how she teased me about being shy, and how we laughed when we caught the katydid on the window in a Dixie cup. And I said to myself, this is silly, my grandfather is going to be all right now that he has gone to the doctor's, and I began to feel the reasons I should surprise Laurie and Matt piling up, like my grandfather wouldn't even have to see me riding to the barn. And my grandmother would say," You have to do what you think is right, baby," and suddenly what I thought was right was to surprise Laurie tomorrow.

And I pushed the covers down with the bottom of my foot and lay there, uncovered, in the big old antique bed, and I turned and looked out the windows. No freighters were moving across the black now, and even the sheets felt sticky and hot.

Friday morning I got a call from Sugar early. I had gotten used to filling in for Sugar at the early feeding when she had to go somewhere since I came by every morning anyway for molasses and oats.

"Will you feed the horses tonight, too, Erin? I get to play a seven o'clock gig at the Topsider Restaurant, a great place."

"Sure," I said.

"Radio says maybe a storm. If it looks like a bad one, let them out in the field. I don't like that barn in an ugly wind."

"All right, Sugar," I told her, and I thought of Shadow who was outside all the time because his barn was no protection it was so full of leaks, and I thought of the shed the wind blew over, upside down on its back.

My grandfather wasn't out of bed when I left, and I looked at the sky because it was a grayer than usual and I knew he would not like to be caught off guard with a storm, but I snuck down the stairs anyway and gave my grandma a hug and started off for Sugar's barn without telling my grandfather about the sky.

None of the leaves were moving on the trees as I walked down Ratt. Still coated with dust from a week without rain, they hung down like so many limp green hands above me. I wiped my upper lip and started to jog, in case of dogs. As I slowed to a walk down the narrow driveway of the Little Farm, past Sugar's old truck which was missing one tire and limping by the side of the fence, I felt fantastic.

At the farmhouse, I picked up an empty pail by the side of the door, knowing no one was home even though the screen door was open. Sugar's whole house smelled of horses, just like Grandpa and the cottage smelled of cigars. Maybe you could tell a whole lot about people from their smells, I decided. A whole lot, and as I put the pail over my arm and started toward the barn I wondered about my smells. I wondered if I smelled like Ivory soap which was

117

the only thing I used all the time or my No More Tears shampoo which I used because I always got shampoo in my eyes.

Across the field the horses grazed, their necks pouring down into the grass as they chewed at short gray summer grass. A wind chime Sugar had tied in the branches clinked softly as a light wind sort of wound its way through the huge maple tree by the corral door. I could barely hear my own footsteps, the grass seemed so wet with humidity that day.

Inside the barn the plank half-door creaked when I opened it to get to the grain. Dipping the coffee can into the barrel, I realized there were only oats in the barrel. Maybe in hurrying to get away Sugar had forgotten to mix in the molasses. Bummer, I thought, I have to mix the molasses and oats myself.

With the empty coffee can still in my hand, I looked for molasses. Wood chips for stall bedding were packed in huge rectangular packages piled in the stall, and I knew there was no molasses in them, so I climbed up on one of the lower packages that stuck out like a shelf to read the wording on some of the smaller packages and containers piled on top. "Revel's Bedding Neutralizer," one read. That wasn't it either. I climbed down and bent over to see if a covered black bucket under a wooden horse held molasses, but it didn't.

This stop was taking me longer than I wanted.

I backed into the middle of the crowded stall as the barn cat suddenly sprang up from the rear and I realized there was space behind the packages of bedding. I scrambled over the top to get into the space.

Then, suddenly, I heard voices outside the door, and for some reason, I dropped down among the packages and I didn't stand up. I don't know why I didn't stand up.

Maybe being in a barn again. Maybe I thought it could be Luddy even though that wouldn't make any sense. Maybe I thought Mrs. Luddy's dog had escaped which was even sillier since her farm was a mile away. Maybe I was just afraid of *empty*. But anyway I sank down onto an upside-down pail and hid in the stall, the unwrapped packages all around me.

"It's too bad," a girl's voice said. "I was afraid she'd be gone."

"I thought when I saw the truck that she'd be somewhere on the farm, and . . ."

"Even Sugar can't drive a truck with three tires, and she locks up her tools, I know that."

"Look, I'm not worried. I'll go into Charlie's Exxon later. It's just a broken starter and it isn't going to go away."

"But to leave the cycle alone . . ."

"It's safe enough in Tracy's ravine."

"We could ride Missy to town and get the part . . ."

"We could, but I don't want to. You know what I want."

I put my hand over my mouth as I recognized Laurie and Matt's voices. For some reason because I didn't stand up right away, I couldn't then. Or it seemed that way, but that was ridiculous, of course I could stand up. I should have let them know I was there. After all it was not like when I hid in the bushes and watched them kiss on the beach. Then I didn't know them together, now they were my two best friends. Later today we would go riding together, three and three, race across the beach together, laugh as the horses scrambled down the bluff together.

Stand up! I shouted to myself.

But I couldn't stand up.

I heard the two of them shuffle across the concrete floor

and open the gate to the last stall where Sugar stored hay, as if they knew exactly where they were going, and I held my stomach and looked up at the barn ceiling. A cobweb covered with dust stretched across the peak in the ceiling from beam to beam. But seeing didn't block out the noises in the last stall.

"Come here," I heard Matt whisper low.

"Matt," Laurie's voice said, soft, with that sweet break in it, but he didn't say anything back. He just made a noise, a soft noise, as if, as if what? I tried to imagine. As if he were kissing her neck? As if he were kissing her mouth? I knew that if I looked through the slats of the stall, I might be able to see, but I couldn't. Still, I could hear those soft sounds, and I hated them.

"I'm glad it turned out like this," he said then, and there were new noises as if they were backing into the steep mountain of hay.

"Me too. I'm always glad," Laurie said, and I thought of what my grandfather said about their sneaking into any empty shed, and I knew Laurie's voice was different. I had never heard that voice before, not from Laurie. Not from Denver. And I wondered what made the difference but only a little because I knew, too. I'm not dumb.

Then there were no voices, only rustling in hay, and I waited for the voices to come back, and for the rustling to stop, and I thought of the little room in the Luddy barn and how the light comes in through the empty window, and I thought of turning and seeing Luddy sprawled in the hay. All of a sudden I screamed inside me, *What are they doing!* and I put my hands over my ears and squeezed them flat, but I could hear the rustling, the soft sounds going on and on, and suddenly I couldn't stand it. I crawled over to the side on my hands and knees so no one could hear me and I looked through the slats.

At first all I could see was the back of Matt's blue denim shirt, but then the two of them twisted around and I could see Laurie's bare arm around Matt's neck. Then I saw Laurie's bare back.

I spun around and, closing my eyes, clamped my hands over my ears so hard I could hardly breathe. But I could still hear the soft hay noises right through my fingers and as I squeezed my eyes shut I heard Laurie say, "I love you, Matt."

"I know," he said.

And I squeezed and squeezed because it was two and two and the barn was empty and full, and real was too hard, and suddenly I pushed the packages of bedding away from me and climbed over the wooden horse and tipped it over and pushed open the stall door. The cat squealed in front of me as I ran out of the stable door.

Behind me I heard Laurie calling, "Erin! Erin! *Wait! Talk to me!*"

No, not Erin, *Montana,* I said to myself and I ran.

Eighteen

*I think I hear Denver calling but I know that's impossible
and so I ride White until I reach the apple-packing building
in the middle of the orchard. Deserted and gray, it looks
like a toy someone has made out of concrete blocks, so
harmless the Barts would never use it for a hideout. A toy!
But it doesn't fool me. I have known all summer what it
is.*

*The long hair on White is sticky wet from running so
far, so I tie her under an apple tree, and start off into the
orchard by the side of the building on foot. I know what I
have to do. Maybe I have known it all along. I can't wait
for Denver this time. Alone, I sneak toward the building,
quickly pulling myself up against an apple tree when I hear
voices. Crouching there, I realize they are inside, noisy
and shouting over the strums of a guitar, but I am good at
voices, at telling what they mean even when I can't see
whose voices they are. I run to the next tree and stop
again, pressing my back flat against the twisted gray
trunk.*

The Barts are smart, I give them that. Who would fig-

ure they'd stop right outside of Dodge City in an old settlers' orchard. I can feel the blood hot in my face as I run to the corner of the building between two windows. No one inside can see me, but I crouch down anyway. I like to play things safe.

But Denver's dead and it isn't easy seeing your sidekick lying outside the hideout with three holes in her side, blood pouring out into the desert sand. I couldn't save her, but I know without knowing that Black Bart did it, and I can get him.

Inside the building I hear singing and shouting, still that guitar. Well, I think, I will give them something to celebrate, and I make a dash for the wood pile and crouch down behind it. Then I pull myself up by my elbows to the edge of the stack when I see a dark shadow slip out of the door and creep into the shadows. I know it's Bart, it's always Bart. I should have known he'd know I was there whether he saw me or not. He and I have been enemies a long time. But I am ready this time.

I get to my knees and raise my arm slow, and I look along the cold steel barrel of my Colt to the tip, when the shadow spins out across the orchard and blasts at me as it spins. Twing, the bullet ricochets not an inch from my ear. Bart. I fire again. He spins away and dashes to the water trough, but I fire again, twing. The shadow leaps and falls behind the trough, still alive.

I drop to the ground, crawling like a cat to a hill of dirt near the end of the wood. Twing. Over my head. Then I creep on my belly, pulling myself inch by inch across the earth to hole up behind the water trough where I can see Bart clear. He doesn't see me go this time, I know that and so I raise my arm and aim just below his black hat, and pick him off. Twing.

He spins into the air, groans, and drops like wet laundry

to the ground. He lies there with blood dripping from his mouth like a dead cat on a road hit by a truck. That is the end of Black Bart, and the guitar is still strumming and the voices still sing and shout inside the little square building. Some hideout, I think. Before I leave I untie all of their horses, knot by knot, and whisper "Git!" and slap one after another on the rump, and they gallop off, their ropes flying as they race through the orchard, and I watch them until all I see are black dots on the horizon like dead flies on a piece of paper.

Then I untie White and, giving her a good slap on the butt so she'll run free, I start back on foot.

Nineteen

The fields are flat and gray in a storm and that afternoon the clouds piled up and crept forward slow as if they were waiting for more to come before they moved on. Everything in the world was still, the leaves, and the clouds, and the fields of black-eyed Susans. I didn't go on to the Luddys'. I didn't want to see Shadow, I didn't want to battle the geese, I didn't want to smell vinegar coming out of Mrs. Luddy's kitchen and I didn't want to see the patch of light in the little room in the barn.

I thought I wanted to see my grandmother, but when I came back the cottage was dark, there was another note: "Have gone to Port Huron. Listen for the bell, and keep the door locked if we don't get home until dark." I sat down in the white rocker like an old lady, I guess, and I didn't feel empty outside, I felt empty inside. Everything had happened, it seemed, but as I sat there, I felt as if there were more to come, and I didn't know what, so I rocked.

I had only been rocking for ten minutes when the phone rang. It was Mrs. Luddy. "You coming over?" she asked.

"Maybe," I said.

"You coming with Steffie?"

"If I come, Mrs. Luddy."

"Well, I can't be there today, but I'll pull the hose out to the barn for you. You put it back in the shed when yer done, hear?" she said. "You be careful, I can't be there today," she said again as if she were warning me or something.

Maybe I was just edgy.

Anyway in the afternoon I tore a piece of bologna out of the package in the refrigerator and was eating it without bread all by myself when I heard voices outside the kitchen window. Danny and Mary, John and Bridie were short-cutting through our yard toward Ratt Road and I am not sure why I ran to the back door, but, I stuffed the bologna in my mouth and got to the door before they passed.

Danny, his one arm around Mary, hugged a big brown bag, and waved to me with it. I guess I would have just waved back, but John was walking with Bridie and as he turned to say something to me, Bridie took his arm and pulled him away, talking to him and laughing with him so he couldn't say anything to me.

It was as if I were waiting for that one little thing to get mad at the whole summer because suddenly, I thought, we would still have bonfires with Grandma Kelly and my grandma and grandpa and the little kids if it weren't for Bridie Kelly, and I would not have fallen off Shadow if it weren't for Bridie Kelly, and John would still have been working on the shed if it weren't for her pulling him off to the fair. And for all I knew it was Bridie Kelly and her town friends breaking into boat houses and porches and scaring everyone—I thought of the grinning boy with the railroad cap, dunking me over and over—and, standing there in the doorway, something exploded in me.

"Hey!" I said and I wasn't afraid, I was smiling and

126

closing the door behind me and thinking I'm going to belong somewhere and Bridie Kelly's not going to stop me!

"Olive Oyl! Where's Blacky?" Danny asked.

Mary looked up at Danny and pecked his chin with her lips. "Shadow, not Blacky, silly."

"Whatever," Danny answered. "He's not with her, is he?"

They all started to pass by me, when I inched up alongside Danny. "I heard the fair was great this year," I said. "The car races sounded outrageous."

"Yeah," Danny said, "you should have come."

Bridie still didn't stop and didn't say anything.

"How's the horse?" Mary asked, her voice sounded gentle really, not as if we were in any war, and I thought she might be an echo but she couldn't have been with Bridie if Bridie were breaking into someone's four-wheel drive. She just couldn't.

"Great!" and I still felt that explosion in me, and when Danny finally said, "Why don't you come down to the Olmstead House with us," I could see the playing cards in his hands along with the brown paper bag and I said, "Sounds good."

See, I'm not so good at beach parties or running with horses or figuring out grandfathers who like wars but I am good at cards. Always have been. And I decided I was going to play cards with Bridie Kelly, and I was going to win. If it was the last thing I did.

The woods were hazy as the five of us walked toward the Olmstead House. Light hardly touched the poison ivy that grew in waves under the trees. By the time we got to the Olmstead House about a mile up the road from Sugar's the clouds had dropped so low they were practically sitting on the roof, which made the house, a tiny old brick Victorian, look really small. It had no top floor anyway, and wild bushes covered the front door and grew right up to the roof. All the building had for as long as I could remember was a name: The Olmstead House, but no one remembered the Olmsteads or if they ever existed at all. It wasn't as if we were breaking into Mrs. Everson's cottage.

One by one we crawled into the back window. Inside, the kitchen air felt cold on my legs and the rust from a slow drip in the sink made the place seem as if no one had ever lived there. There was no electricity, just gray light that sort of sifted in through yellowy torn lace curtains at the side window. But there were thick, half-melted candles, and Bridie lit two, while we all sat on these ghost chairs covered with old gray sheets.

Danny kept the brown bag tucked behind him as if it had some big mystery in it and Mary sat down in front of him, leaning against his knees. I knew John was looking at me but I didn't look back. Instead I looked at the bag and wondered what was in it. And I thought of the bottles Jim Anders kept finding all over. Whatever was in it was too big to be cigarettes. I felt as if I were looking into the crack again and I wondered if I was already too far on the other side to get across. I guess I figured right then I had to be part of whatever was in that bag. Whether I liked it or not.

But we played cards first.

"Spit," Bridie decided. She had forgotten that other summers I had been great at "spit." A kind of four-person solitaire, it can be wild and fast, the idea being to get rid of your cards.

"Anything's fair," she added.

"What does that mean!" Danny said, practically shouting.

"Oh, nothing," she laughed. "Just house rules." Why he let her boss even him around I couldn't understand.

"House rules," he repeated but he didn't say any more.

I knew as soon as we started what it meant. It meant Bridie was out to win too and it didn't matter how hard she slapped, or what pile she grabbed away. All right, I thought to myself. Anything's fair. Everyone must have felt the same because suddenly no one was speaking.

We played double deck. Hands whipped red queens to black jacks. Someone slapped a nine down on a ten to stop Danny when he got hot. Then we tried to stop Mary. I raked the cards into my pile with my fingertips without even stacking them so I didn't have to stop.

Early I slapped a red jack on John's black ten before he could touch his card. We still were not looking at each other.

"Man, Olive, you're quick," Danny said.

"Getting better," I said as if I had just told Shadow to move his big butt over, not shy. Anything's fair.

The hands slapped in front of me, even as I felt the beads of sweat forming under my arms and rolling cold down my side. A rumble of thunder didn't stop me, although the tiny one-room house grew darker. I knew I was getting rid of more and more cards and I didn't slow down.

"Hey," Mary squealed, "she's only got about eight cards left."

And I saw Bridie look up, but she didn't say anything. She just leaned over farther, her face closer to the cards.

I whipped a red ten on her black jack before she could get her next card out.

"You're hot, Erin," Danny said.

John said nothing, but I didn't look to see what his *face* said because I didn't take my eyes off the piles of cards in front of me. I wanted to win. And card after card, I slapped down, beating Danny to the pile, beating Mary, beating John and trying to beat Bridie. But Bridie wanted to win, too.

"I don't love this," Danny laughed. I loved it.

When I played a black nine, Bridie whipped her ten under it even though my nine had been down, and grinned.

All right, I said to myself. All right. I didn't take my eyes off the cards, and an instant later I slapped a nine, ten before Bridie could breathe, then I beat her to a red four. And a black nine, getting rid of an eight, a seven a six. I was like a machine gun, and the others could hardly stay in the game, the two of us were so quick, because something was going on they didn't really understand.

"Hey, you guys," Danny said, sitting back with his cards folded in his hands. "You crazy?"

Neither of us looked at him. I had one card, a red six, to get rid of, but of course Bridie didn't know that. She had two cards. As Danny reshuffled the tiny pack and turned them over, I caught sight of a black seven on the bottom, the card I needed to go out. I started to say something about it, then I just sat forward, ready. All's fair.

I leaned forward to spring. When Danny reset the pile, I slapped the red six on before Bridie even had a chance to pick her cards up, and raked my fingernail across her wrist.

"Hey, lady!" Bridie shrieked, stopping completely. There was electricity in the room.

"Sorry," I sat back, sort of panting, looking at the fresh blood on her arm.

"This isn't a life and death thing, you know," Bridie said, her chin pushing out on each word, a red eight cupped in her hand.

"I didn't say it was."

"You act like it, girl." Bridie sucked the blood off her arm.

"Sorry," I said, suddenly glad the room was growing darker because I could feel the blood rush into my cheeks.

"You are too good to come with us all summer, then suddenly, you're just one of the gang, aren't you?"

I just looked at her. Is that what she thought? *I thought I was too good?* I looked at John, sure he'd stick up for me then, but he was whispering into Bridie's ear. I should have guessed when he had to make a choice who he would side with. Just because we shared an old boat and a few geese didn't mean we were anything special to each other. I felt myself pushing back against the old faded wallpaper, sorry that I had come, but realizing that I finally knew what Bridie really was, an empty balloon, showy with nothing inside.

"Well," Bridie went on, if she wasn't going to win at cards, she was going to win at something. "When have we seen her last? She's such a big shot, hanging out with Sugar or Laurie or . . ."

"Oh, can it, Bridie!" Danny said.

"No, I won't *can* it!"

"Maybe you will, Bridie!" her brother said, taking her arm.

She pulled away really mad. "Then you don't know me, Danny!" she shouted at him.

I shouldn't have come, and I felt the wall cold against my back when a shadow crossed the window and a face peered in.

"Erin here?" Steffie asked, one pigtail dropping over the inside of the window as she looked in.

Bridie stopped speaking, but Danny answered, "Maybe."

"Well, come on, Erin!" she said in her squeaky voice. "Aren't we going to hose Shadow down, and Sugar says the horses need to be fed before we put them out if it storms and . . ."

"I'm not coming."

"Come on, Erin," Steffie ordered. And I could feel my face get hot hearing her talk to me that way. As if she were someone's mother!

Bridie started to laugh hard and look at John, happy as anything that Steffie was doing this to me. "I guess I forgot about Erin's little Steffie," Bridie said.

"You coming, Erin?" Steffie ignored her and ran around to the front door and looked through the torn screen at us.

"No, Steffie, I'm not," I heard myself say because I wasn't leaving until I got into the brown bag along with everyone else.

"Erin!" she whined.

"Go on, Stef," John said to her. "Go home.

"No one's home."

"Go visit Billy." I knew her friend Billy lived down the beach.

"But it's going to rain."

"Steffie," John said, "go on, get lost." And she turned, gave me a last begging look and when I didn't say anything, started running through the weeds toward Ratt. I felt like running after her to tell her I'd see her later, or something, but the truth is, I didn't.

The room had grown dark even though it was only five o'clock, and there was a kind of quiet outside, so I knew the storm was coming, but Danny began to open the bag, unrolling the crumpled top with his fingers. What he had was something in a big bottle, something clear, and he said, "Let's forget this card game, Erin, you're the winner." That didn't make Bridie happy and she grabbed the bottle from him, unscrewed the cap and tipped it into her mouth. Then she handed it across John to me, as if she were so sure I wouldn't take it. But she didn't know me, and I took it and poured it into my mouth. It was like fire going down my throat and I started to cough and my eyes teared even though I fought it.

"You sure you want this?" Bridie mocked but I noticed her eyes were teary too.

"Why not?" I said because I was sick of being nowhere.

John shook his head and sat back stacking the cards and Danny and Mary started to laugh as some of whatever it was spilled down the front of her.

After I had drunk another sip or two, or maybe three, I felt a kind of buzzing in my head that I didn't like, because I didn't know what it was, but I also heard a crack of thunder. When the bottle came to me, I started to take another drink and a peal of thunder rolled over the top of the house so close the house shook.

We all stopped and Danny held the bottle as if he were frozen. "Hey," he said, looking up at the ceiling as if it were going to come apart. "Let's get out of here. There's going to be a big one."

A big one. John looked across at me for the first time as if he were wondering how I was, and I saw him, but my head was foggier than I wanted it to be and I wanted to hear what was happening outside so I couldn't make a mistake.

"Want a last one?" Danny said, searching for the bag and handing the bottle to me at the same time, but suddenly I didn't even know why I was there! I shook my head. My head was full of the storm, and I knew Danny was right. Something big was coming. All that thunder and heat and no rain was no good. The sky wanted to explode from it.

"It's two weather fronts," I said out loud. The others

scrambled to pull on their shoes and pick up their cards, and I remembered Sugar's horses were trapped in the barn. While they scrambled to find their sneakers and things, I stood up and ran to the kitchen door, stumbling out the doorway.

"Is it a tornado?" Mary called after me. "Is that what it is?"

I didn't know. I just ran down Ratt. I didn't notice John and Bridie were behind me until the beginning of Sugar's fence.

Twenty

The sky looked like a boiling cauldron as I cut through the orchard to get to Sugar's barn. I kept thinking of the shed the wind had turned over. Of course, that was three-sided and it turned over because the wind couldn't get out, but weather is in my bones, and I knew without Sugar telling me that horses are better outside in a tornado where they will have a chance to outrun the flying wood and metal that a funnel sucks up and spits into the air.

I leapt across the ditch into the furrows that stretched through the orchard, my feet sinking into soft dirt. Behind me I could hear John running, and ahead I saw Sugar's barn. It looked small with all the gray sky behind it, just a long tin-covered shack. The gate to it had sort of yawned open.

At the fence I climbed over, catching my shorts on a barb, but, ripping my pant leg off of it, I jumped down and kept running.

"Hey," John panted as we ran across the uneven furrows. "It's just a thunderstorm!"

A sharp crack of light answered him, splitting the sky

and turning the gray field white. At the gate, I lifted it with both hands and pulled it wide open. Missy whinnied inside the barn and the cat sprang in front of me as I started down the aisle that ran through the stable.

"Turn them all out," I said. John ran for the pony. Missy was nervous, stamping in front of her gate, but, squeezing into her stall, I grabbed her halter and, pushing the gate open with my foot, I ran her out into the corral where the gate was still open. There I gave her a slap and sent her running out into the open field where the wind was carrying the first sprinkles of the storm.

Inside, I heard John shout, "Get a knife!"

As I ran in, Bridie was running in the other door. "What do you need?" she shouted. The wind was rushing through the stable like a noisy swarm of something living.

"Nothing," I shouted back and slipped into the stall with John.

"I can help, you know!" Bridie hollered out, following me, but I didn't answer her.

"His rope is tangled on the water bucket!" John said, working on it. I turned to run for something to cut it, when Bridie pulled a small penknife out of her hip pocket. I started to go around her when this kind of creepy moan of air wound through the barn and I grabbed the knife and handed it to John.

Then I ran to the foal in the stall next to the feed. As I slipped through the gate, it jumped away from me on spindly legs. "Easy," I whispered and, grabbing its rope bridle, I led it out. When I turned to kick the gate open, though, the foal suddenly pulled away, and skittered toward the stable door that led out to the unfenced field.

Bridie had just come running back into the barn, John was at the feed barrels, and for a moment the three of us just stood there in the empty barn and a flash of lightning lit the barn and the foal, frozen in the open doorway. *We had to catch it before it got to that unfenced field.* Panicky, I inched slowly toward it from the left while John moved toward it from the right. You couldn't even hear our feet because the wind tunneled through the middle of the stable, and we didn't see Bridie back out the other stable door.

"Easy, baby," I cooed. I knew how Sugar felt about it.

The tack and buckets and saddles seemed like gray shadows as I moved through them, my hand straight out in front of me. Then, within two feet I lurched at the rope halter, but the foal jumped sideways and ran out the open doorway. A long roll of thunder ripped the sky open as the foal started toward the driveway.

But a shadow suddenly jumped off the barbed-wire fence, its arms outspread like an eagle or something, and stopped in front of the open driveway blocking the foal. Bridie.

"Ahhhhh!" she said out loud, sweeping her arms up and down and the foal stopped, sort of startled.

As John crept slowly toward the little animal, I fell back into the feed stall and pushed some oats into a small coffee can. Then I walked back toward the foal, slow, shaking the coffee can gently in front of me.

The foal's ears twitched forward as it heard the familiar sound of the oats brushing against the sides of the can. I stuck the can out. The foal looked suspiciously at it, then lurched away in Bridie's direction.

But Bridie put her arms up again, spreading her fingers and arms and waving them like wings, and the foal stopped short. I shook the can again. Behind it, I could see dark clouds coming up behind Sugar's farmhouse. *We were in a hurry.* The foal's nostrils flared, and the whites of its eyes became crescents as I shook the can again, and then all at once the little animal turned its spindly legs toward me, hopping playfully like a goat toward the can. I could hardly believe it.

Suddenly, a lightning streak broke over the pond, lighting the foal and our hair and shirts, and I threw the can clanking down, and, grabbing the halter, ran the foal through the barn and out into the fenced-in field.

The first drops of rain fell on my shoulders as I ran back toward the wide mouth of the barn, and I wondered if tornados came with the first rain.

"Let's get out of here!" John shouted.

"I'm going to Shadow," I said and started out.

"You crazy? Get to a basement," John said. You went to a basement to escape a tornado. "You can't do anything for Shadow! He's outside!" he said. "He'll be okay!"

"Come on, you guys!" Bridie shouted at us. The wind was beginning to pick up tiny circles of leaves and the barn cat sprinted in front of John to a hole under the farmhouse as the rain started pouring down in sheets that flew sideways across the field. I looked up at the sky, letting the rain pour hard and warm on my face and shoulders.

"Suit yourself, we're going," John shouted as he took Bridie's arm and pushed her into a run down the driveway without me.

For a minute I didn't know what to do and I stood, watching them run hunched over, down the driveway.

"Come on, Erin," Bridie turned and shouted a last time. *"Please, come!"*

And I started running after them because I figured if anyone could outrun a tornado, Shadow could.

The rain pushed me as I ran down the road, throwing wet spikes of water at my neck and backs of my legs. I had never heard a storm whistle before like that, the wind winding through the branches around me, as if it were looking for something.

"Is it a tornado?" Bridie shouted, still running.

"I don't know," I shouted back.

"Run faster," John kept saying, falling back to wait every few seconds. But at the cutoff through the sumach trees, he said, "Get to Mary's basement." The Tracys had one of the only basements on the bluff. John started to run the other way.

Bridie stopped. "Where are you going?" she called after him, looking really scared. The wind was whipping around her.

"To find Steffie!"

"Where's Steffie?" I said, stopping next to her. I had forgotten Steffie!

"Maybe home. Maybe Billy's."

"Oh," I started after him without even thinking. I couldn't not go after Steffie again.

"No," John said when he saw me coming through the sumach. *"The Tracys' basement!"* he shouted even as he kept running toward the bluff.

"You can't go down on the beach in this!" I shouted, and I knew I had to let him go because I realized there wasn't time for words, and he disappeared down the stairs and I heard myself think there's no time to get to anyone's basement, just a southwest corner, and I found myself running into a wall of rain and branches without anywhere to go.

Then all at once I knew.

"John!" I yelled to where he had disappeared. "The foundation!" The foundation where the cottage used to stand was only a few feet away, but I knew John hadn't heard me, and I knew there was no basement at the Mullin cottage.

Bridie and I pulled branches aside as we made our way through dripping red sumach bushes, then we climbed into the cobblestone foundation and ran, crouched, across the weeds growing in the rubble of broken glass and stones. Finally we sank into the southwest corner.

A sharp piece of concrete poked into my back but I stayed flattened against the stone, huddled next to Bridie. The wind was full of rain and neither of us said anything, as if we were waiting for some of it to snatch us, and I thought, we are going to die. People all over not expecting this are going to die. Because people always die in tornados: William Smith, age twelve, Mary Jones, age seven, the papers always said. And I wondered where Steffie was and my grandmother and grandfather and, I thought, what will a wind do to their little Dodge car putzing down the highway, and I worried about crazy things like my grandfather's binoculars out on the wicker table in the cottage, and I thought it was crazy that I was huddling there in a storm with Bridie Kelly whom I hated and I looked at her and her whole face was soft and white as if she were going to cry and I didn't hate her at all.

She saw me looking at her. "It's my mom and dad," she got out over the wind, "and Grandma Kelly and the kids," and she did everything she could to stop herself from crying and she wasn't an empty balloon.

"You've got a basement!" I said.

"They went picnicking . . . at the park."

I didn't know.

"They're not on the beach . . . and . . . Bridie . . . Kellys aren't like other people! . . . They'll . . . be . . . okay!" and I was practically shouting over the wind sounds, and for the first time I thought of Laurie. And I wondered if Matt got his starter switch or if his motorcycle were still down in the ravine. And I hoped the two of them were safe at the gas station in town, I hoped hard, and Bridie took my arm and the two of us held onto each other, squeezing against the wind.

Twenty-one

I never thought of leaving the foundation. After all, I was safe, in the southwest corner, but we had only been in the rubble for a few minutes when over the wind I heard a siren. Two long whistles meant the end of a tornado warning, but this siren whined on and on and closer and closer, and all of a sudden I started crawling across the concrete rubble. I just knew it was an ambulance or the police car and, in my bones, I knew it had to do with my grandfather and I felt sick in the bottom of my stomach because I just knew he was dead. No matter what kind of a war we were fighting, I didn't want my grandpa to be dead.

"It's Grandpa," I whispered, looking back at Bridie before I climbed out of the foundation, the wind swirling around my feet.

"Erin, you don't know that!"

"I know it, Bridie. Stay . . . I'll be back." She just had to believe me quickly. There wasn't any time for more words.

But out on the driveway to the cottage I didn't see any ambulance or police car. Or even hear one. The siren and whatever it belonged to had disappeared. I ran toward the bluff, crazily, looking for something—I didn't know what—but there was only wind. And as I passed the cottage it seemed to shudder, the limbs of the pine trees swinging wildly in front of it, and I had nearly reached the stairs to the beach when, through all the sounds, I heard my name and saw Laurie turning the corner of the porch.

"Erin! Have you seen Matt?" she screamed, her hair blowing across her face, strands catching in her mouth.

"No!" I shouted back.

"He left me to go to town, but . . . hours ago. God, he must have gotten trapped on the beach fixing his bike, and . . ." Still facing me, she started backing down the trail toward the Tracy's Point.

"Laurie, you can't go down there!" The Point was the wildest part in a storm.

"I have to, Erin," she said.

Catching up to her, I reached her sleeve. "You can't!"

"He needs me, Erin," she said and, pulling away, she started running down the trail, her hair flying behind her in the crazy wind.

I started after her then stopped, "But, Laurie," I cried. "I need you too. Didn't you know that, Laurie? *Didn't you remember?*"

But she had disappeared into the storm. It had stolen her, like the sirens, and I stood there hearing and feeling nothing. Until I realized a bell was ringing. *The pumphouse bell.* And I started running away from the trail, toward the stairs, forgetting the pumphouse was on the beach too, just thinking over and over, "Save the pumphouse, save the cottage."

Slick from the rain, the stairs were slippery, and I held onto the rail, ducking into the wet wind as if that would help. Twigs snapped against my legs, and the rain began to feel colder, and I wondered if that was when a tornado comes: when the rain turns cold. But as I reached the bottom stairs, I knew why the bell was ringing.

Waves rolling in like gray metal cylinders had torn the entire beach away, leaving rocks and huge boulders exposed where sand used to be and leaving a broken water pipe exposed. When it broke in two, I don't know, but I could see the part in the lake being heaved around by waves, a tiny telescope eye that disappeared then rose again with each new swell.

I didn't even think about whether I should go into the lake or not. No one was there but me, and I had to get the end of the pipe, and I started wading in, when a wave rolled up like a great gray giant hunched over the beach. When I saw it coming at me, I ran back to escape and I waited, until it slunk back out. When I thought the water was low enough, I ran out again. I could see the pipe floating on top of the short calm, and I ran for it, the water splashing around my legs, when the gray giant came roaring at me again. And I felt a kind of panic because I thought, I can't get that pipe, and if the water were strong and wild enough to take the pipe, the pumphouse would go next.

I backed up against the bluff as the giant jumped at me, letting the froth slide down my ankles without moving as it slunk back. My chest felt squeezed as if the seams of my body had been sewn too tight and they were going to burst open. I could feel tears running out of my eyes even though I wasn't sad, when I heard a voice over the shushing water.

"Erin!" I heard the voice call from way down the beach, and it was John running through the tips of the waves. "Erin!" he called and ducked under the willow tree whose roots were so exposed the water was swirling under the root fingers.

And I waved. "Over here," I shouted. "John! Over here!" And I pointed at the pipe.

"Forget it!" he said, but he didn't understand. I couldn't forget it. I started to go back into the waves without him, but he waded in after me, and we didn't run away when the gray giant came again, we stood there, locking our legs. When I could see the telescope eye of the pipe swing toward us, we both jumped at it, my hand touched it, and I saw him on the other side. I wished that I could touch the bottom, but the giant had pulled the bottom out from under me, and the water was beating against my face until I thought I would have to let go.

But our hands had the pipe, and we hung on and when the giant slunk out this time, we were left lying on the beach scraping across the sand. As John got to his knees to reach the beach end of the pipe, I saw a figure climbing down the bluff. I couldn't believe it. It was my grandfather, and I thought he should be in the foundation or somewhere safe, but he didn't look sick at all as he sprang through the pine trees.

"Leave it!" he shouted, and John stood up with the beach end of the pipe still in his hand, water draining off his shorts and shirt, shaking.

And I wouldn't let go of the lake end. I crawled up closer on the beach before the giant could get me, but I hung onto the pipe.

"Erin! John!" my grandfather shouted again. "Let go of that pipe! Get over here!" He wasn't even looking at the pumphouse, and the waves were grabbing at the stones nearest to it, and the bell was ringing and ringing. The door had swung open, and crazily I wondered why the lock hadn't held, but, just then, I looked up and I saw a black cloud and I heard a queer noise I've never heard before in the sky. I dropped the pipe, and John and I scrambled up the bank, tearing at anything that was rooted, poison ivy, small pine trees, raspberry bushes. I didn't even feel the scratches, I just heard the sound in the sky screaming as if finally it were going to blow itself up. *Tornado.*

Facedown on the side of the bluff, we burrowed into the bramble alongside my grandfather, who reached over and pressed his hand down over mine, and John was next to me and the three of us were buried there, waiting, when out of the corner of my eye I saw this black blur coming down the stairs. Matt.

"Get down!" my grandfather yelled at him without lifting his head.

"Screw it!" Matt shouted back, stumbling and slipping down the long red stairs because the wind was blowing so hard he could hardly stand upright, and I realized his bike must still be down there and so was Laurie.

"Fool!" my grandfather shouted, red-faced, and pushing himself up, he crouched across the bluff toward him. "The . . . sky," he got out, and I realized my grandfather was trying to warn him, too, but Matt jumped down the last ten steps right into the waves.

"For God's sake," my grandfather tried. The wind was whining louder and louder and my grandfather, his face absolutely pale, leapt over the brush to where we were and threw himself across both of us, burying my face in the brush. I tasted dirt in my mouth.

Then the whine grew weird, like a moan spiraling down from the sky above me, and I prayed, help us, help please, and the new dark wind started down and every tree seemed to hold its breath. Then it let go. Twigs and leaves and small things stung my legs and the air grew dark and the pumphouse creaked and suddenly something small broke loose and went flying across the bank crashing against a tree, loud, and I heard the roof rattle as if it were being pulled and pulled like a pulse. Then I heard something big snap and I turned my head without lifting it.

Something like a huge, moving cloud *was picking the whole pumphouse up,* slowly, as if it were a heavy dollhouse, right off the concrete, slow, right over the rocks, over the fence up ten feet, twenty feet in the air! Then the cloud sucked up the waves beneath it like a movie running backwards. A life jacket and some clothes fell out of the pumphouse right into the air and, just as suddenly, the whole pumphouse fell, landing in the shallow water, almost bent in two.

What, I thought to myself, could ever be that strong!

Then the boiling cloud, like a finger finished pointing, pulled itself up into the sky, and out over the lake, it grew stubbier and stubbier and finally disappeared up in the layer of clouds and, though it was lighter now, the rain really began, pouring down in cold sheets.

"My God," my grandfather whispered without moving. "I . . . I had no idea."

And John turned over, the rain falling on him, looking at the lake, his back against the bluff. My legs and arms stung as if needles had pricked them. I didn't know why we and the bushes and trees on the bluff were even there.

Then, all at once, John pointed down toward the crumpled pumphouse. "Look," he said. Sticking out from under the corner of the building, I saw what looked like a leg wearing blue denim. *The falling clothes.* Grandfather saw it, too, and with the rain streaming down our faces, the three of us started slowly down the bank, pulling aside the bushes, which I realized for the first time had no leaves at all and were all bent in one direction.

At the building, my grandfather and John and I waded through the waves and tried to push the corner aside. The whole building, only a tin shell now, had nothing in it, no pump, no bell, but we couldn't move it. Since the door was on its side, my grandfather climbed into the window, and I climbed in after him, and as I dropped down off the sill after my grandfather, I saw Mr. Luddy in a yellow shirt lying in the water with the waves seeping over him, then seeping back. The jagged metal corner of the pumphouse had opened the side of his head and he was blue.

I had never seen anyone who was blue before.

"Who is he?" my grandfather asked, surprised.

"Leon Luddy," John said from the window, and the waves washed over Mr. Luddy again, floating the shirt collar around his neck back and forth like the gills of a dead fish.

"My God, that's why the bell was ringing. He must have electrocuted himself in the pumphouse . . . Erin, go tell your grandmother to call the police," and I ran over to the stairs and, climbing up, I wondered if Mr. Luddy used to have a red shirt, too, and I knew who had been breaking into the boat houses and cottages.

I didn't think then about Matt and his bike and Laurie, and whether they had found each other before the tornado came.

Twenty-two

The sirens seemed to wail in the night when the ambulance and police car drove down the ravine road between our house and the Mullins' to get as close as they could to the pumphouse. In a yellow rain slicker, Jim Anders climbed out of the first car and said he thought it was Grandma Kelly again because the first siren had been for Grandma Kelly who had had a heart attack, and when I tried to find out more he was already hurrying down toward the beach. "She was resting fine right at the cottage when I left her," he said. "Refused to be taken anywhere else."

When a patrolman from Crosley finally brought Mrs. Luddy over to the beach a few minutes later, my grandmother was the one who went right over to her and took her arm, but Mrs. Luddy wasn't even sad, it seemed. Instead she was really mad and said it served Mr. Luddy right, that he spent more time in his truck than at home or working, him and his damned beer, she said, bottles all over, she said, good riddance, she said. And I thought, the world is crazy—turned upside down.

But then I wondered if Mrs. Luddy were telling the

truth, because when she came down to the waterfront a flashlight flashed on her face and I could see that it wasn't shiny and rosy anymore, it was white and her eyes were red all around the rims as if she had been crying and crying, and she looked right at me, but didn't seem even to recognize me.

And I asked Officer Anders before he drove away if everyone else was all right and he said yes, but Littleton was in pieces, that's what he said, "Beams right through the General Store window," and he said, "Someone found the headless dummy down on the highway."

Then I saw Mrs. Kelly and Sugar walking past all the cars down the beach toward Tracy's ravine, real fast, and I didn't know why they were going down the beach if everyone else was all right.

"Mrs. Kelly," I called, "everyone all right?"

But she was running with some blankets so she didn't answer at all and the light from the flashlight wobbled out in front of her.

I just waited out on the landing because in my bones I had a terrible feeling Jim Anders didn't know everything. My grandfather came out once and put his cap backwards on me, "Come on, Erin," he said, but I wouldn't leave.

It was completely stone dark when I heard the voice and saw the jiggling flashlight showing the way to people carrying someone in a white blanket, like a sling.

It had to be Laurie or Matt and the blanket covered almost all of whoever it was. Even the head. I just froze there.

"Careful!" I heard Mrs. Kelly whisper.

And I couldn't ask anything, I just ran down the stairs and across the sand, and looked into the blanket and saw Laurie's head jiggling from side to side like the head of a dead bird or something.

"Careful!" Mrs. Kelly said again, and I thought why be careful now, and I could feel it hot behind my eyes when Mrs. Kelly added softly, "Watch that leg!"

Leg! I started to run alongside the blanket sling and the light fell on Laurie's face, all pale but squinting, *squinting*, as if something hurt her bad. Matt was carrying one of the ends of the blanket, but I don't think anyone saw me in the dark. "Her right leg may be shattered," someone said, "then you shouldn't have moved her," someone else said. But I started to laugh and cry at the same time. Her *leg*, I thought, running beside her, just *her leg*.

The ambulance rode right over the beach to get to where they set her down in the blanket sling and someone must have radioed somewhere, because when I went back up the bluff the Calleys were parking in our backyard, and when I saw Matt Calley climbing in his father's car later, his cheeks were smeared and wet, and he looked sort dazed, almost like a little boy.

My grandma stayed to talk to Mr. Kelly and found out Laurie had made it to the cycle in the ravine and Matt had too, but that a small tornado had spun right down into the ravine and broken bushes and branches and trees like a hand squeezing a fistful of pick-up sticks or something. A giant tree, I don't know what kind, was pulled over and, see, Laurie and Matt couldn't run anywhere, not through all the bramble in the ravine and the awful wind. Another foot, Mrs. Kelly told my mother, and it would have fallen across the two of them. We found out later the leg had been broken in three places—shattered.

"Erin," my grandmother said to me, because with all the lights flashing and people shouting to "get out of the way" or to "let us through," I crawled up on the porch and watched. "It's going to be okay, you know," But I just nodded and kept sitting there numb because I didn't really think summer would ever be the same again. How could it be.

And after all the cars and trucks that had followed the two ambulances left, screeching and churning out of the fields around our cottage, I went up to bed and lay across it, alone, and listened to freighter horns still hooting. My grandfather came into my room without turning on the light and stroked my hair like he used to when I was a little girl. He thought I was asleep.

In the morning my grandma borrowed three pails of water from the Mullins because we had no water, and I splashed some of it cold over my face before breakfast, but I didn't eat. I kept standing by the old shed just looking at the Kellys', even though I knew they had taken Laurie to the hospital. Just kept standing.

Then all of a sudden I started down the driveway toward Ratt. Just to walk, I thought. My grandparents didn't stop me, and I started thinking a lot of things that weren't connected, like about where Mrs. Luddy had slept last night and if she had called Liebling, her German shepherd, into bed with her just to feel something warm, and I wondered if Shadow had outrun the storm and if the barn was still standing.

The sky had cleared, the fronts had passed, and the air squeezing inside my collar was cool. Usually I hate a north wind because it steals summer and blows in cold water from the center of Lake Huron and no one can swim, but this time the cold air meant the storm was over and it felt good.

Mrs. Luddy was still in bed, I guess, because the brown stained shades in her bedroom were pulled down. Suddenly I didn't want to know what I'd find in the barnyard. I wanted to turn back, but I made myself go at least to the barn, and I found Shadow practically where I had left him, but pulling leaves off a huge maple tree that had been ripped right out of the ground in the storm.

Dropping my jacket, I ran to him and he didn't bolt or anything, he just swung his head around as if to say, "Where've you been?" and I grabbed him around the shoulders and hugged him, my head on his big warm chest. A lot of people say horses don't know people, not really, but he didn't move an inch and when I scratched him around the shoulders with my fingertips he rippled his skin as if he liked it.

I guess I decided then that I'd take him down to the beach, by myself, and he must have run for his life during the storm because he was a real gentleman for me walking down Ratt Road. "You're a good guy," I told him, and scratched his neck as we walked. He even left the black-eyed Susans alone.

To cross the highway, I climbed off him, then walked him down the ravine trail to the lake just to be safe. The sun had come out, too bright to look at, and I climbed back on him and started across the shallow waves toward the jetty. Shadow splashed the waves as if he couldn't imagine what this stuff was that he was walking through. Every so often he would stomp the water just to figure it out. I'm not sure even now what I expected to find there. It was almost as if once I saw the beach I would know what was left of summer.

But I must have been riding toward the ravine where the boat was hidden all the time because that's where I ended up, and I looked into the ravine as far as I could without getting off. Not that I could actually see John's dory sloop, though I thought I saw the can of blue paint through the trees still sitting on the seat. Then I tied Shadow to a poplar tree and started to walk out on the beach alone. I didn't expect to see anyone else there, I don't think.

The beach was a mess, branches sheared off and strewn everywhere, a part of a tire, small slivers of wood. Gulls swept along the point, then coasted back up onto new cold currents of air. They didn't seem to notice the world had broken apart.

I was just walking, empty like that, when two hands came up behind me and touched my shoulders and it was John. I was so glad to see him that I started to cry. I don't know why seeing him did that to me, but it did, and then, before I really knew it, we were hugging each other. Tight. You know? As if we were keeping something away. And I felt so warm there with our arms around each other. And when we pulled away, he took my hand, tight in his, and we walked out on the rock jetty without saying anything.

Oh, I wanted to say, I am really glad you're here, John, but I said, "I think your boat's all right."

"I know," he said, "I came down before breakfast." Then he looked at me as if he wanted to put his arms around me again, but he said, "They think Grandma Kelly's going to be all right. She's just lost some control."

"They say she wouldn't get off the rocker through half the storm," he went on. "Mr. Kelly had to pick her up and move her to the basement. They only got her to the hospital this morning."

I could see Grandma Kelly fighting Mr. Kelly as he carried her. "Did someone take Henry to the hospital with her?" I had hardly spoken since the night before, and words felt strange in my mouth. Cottony.

"Henry?"

"Her walker."

John smiled. "Oh, yeah."

"I hope she gets to use him," I said and I had that empty feeling again, so I said quickly, "And Steffie?" I knew what we weren't saying.

"She's good, she was under her bed wrapped in a blanket, not at Billy's."

"I'm so glad," I said. I knew the wind hadn't damaged the Mullin place. And I realized I loved Steffie even if she was eight years old and full of poison ivy. "She's a friend, you know."

He nodded.

"And Danny and Mary are okay."

He nodded, "And Bridie."

Then neither one of us spoke.

"About Laurie, Erin."

I felt my insides turn, but I said, "It's okay, John. I know her. She'll be okay. I know!"

"You're right." Then he stared at his feet. "I keep seeing those waves, you know? It's almost as if I am on a ship and the ground won't stop moving."

And I nodded.

"We could have been killed, Erin," he added, shaking his head slowly as if he could hardly believe it.

And I thought of Luddy. There were so many things I wanted to say but for some reason all I said was, "Aren't your legs cold?" I had buried myself in my parka and sweatpants and could still feel the wind on my arms and back.

He shook his head no, but I didn't know how that could be when his legs were bare and all he had on were Adidas shorts and a windbreaker.

We walked out to the very tip of the jetty, the wind icy out there.

"It'll all go back together," he said. The wind was blowing a mist of water across us.

I looked up at him.

"Summer," he said.

Then he looked at me for a minute and kissed me so soft, on the lips. And I thought, he even smells good, like fresh air.

Then we started walking again.

"I thought it was Matt when I saw the body floating. I didn't really see which direction he had run."

"I know."

"And Luddy had been the one breaking into the summer side, your grandfather was right."

"I heard that too."

"I've been thinking, maybe it was hard for him seeing what he couldn't have . . . anyway, it wasn't Matt."

"I'm glad," I admitted.

"Really?" John said.

"Really."

"They say when they found Matt and Laurie, they were huddled in the ravine together with the bike like three kids, him, Laurie and his bike."

"I think my grandfather likes Matt," I said. I hadn't really known it before I said it.

"Maybe he's like your grandfather used to be, you know." He grinned. "From what I hear, your grandfather wasn't exactly the sweet kid on the block."

I shrugged. Maybe. And we walked again, not talking for the longest time, and all at once I looked across at him. "You can do it again, if you want." At first he didn't know what I meant, then standing in front of me, he put his hand around the back of my neck and bent over and kissed me lightly again, and I looked up at him, it felt like for the first time.

For a second I felt guilty, as if I shouldn't feel good when everything had broken apart, Littleton, Laurie,

Luddy, and maybe he could read my mind, because all of a sudden he took my hand again and led me back through the ravine to the boat. The boat had weathered the storm, though there were twigs and leaves everywhere around it, and we climbed in by the center board.

After a few seconds, just sitting there, saying nothing, he looked into his hands. "Look, Erin, maybe we could write this fall," he said.

"Maybe," I said.

"We've got a lot to talk about."

"Argue about," I said, half smiling.

"Talk . . . about this summer."

"About Bridie," I said and narrowed my eyes at him. I was teasing.

"Haven't you figured out yet that there is nothing to say about Bridie? She's my friend, and probably always will be. Hey, she's a terrific kid but . . ." And he must have run out of words because he pulled me beside him and, nodding his head to something I couldn't see, he turned and put his hand on the tiller.

"I think we should go to Canada," he said and bent over, squinting through the trees toward the lake.

"Yes?" I said, trying to smile, and I sat closer to him. "All right. Let's go," and I thought, you've got to dream something before it can happen, don't you? And I looked through the branches toward the beach at Shadow tied down below and he swung his head up at us sitting in the boat, half buried in the sand.

Before I went to bed that night, my grandmother sat on the side of the bed, the springs squeaking gently.

"About 'real,' Grandma," I told her. "It was there all the time."

"I know, dear," she started rubbing my back.

"On both sides of the highway . . ."

"Yes."

"It's just being ready to be part of it."

Later that night I heard my grandmother and grand-father arguing about if my grandfather put in a well, whether he would dig the hole himself or not. My grand-mother said he could go right ahead, but he could drive himself to the hospital if he did. And I thought to myself maybe everything changes, but I was glad that night that some things change slow. Like the two of them. And I stood up on the bed, holding on to the brass bedpost, and looked out the high windows at the Mullin cottage.

There were no lights on in it, and John's bike was lean-ing up against the moonlit cottage porch. Over the trees beyond the cottage I could see the rooftop of the Kellys'. "Kelly," I whispered out loud, "Kelly." I loved that name and all of them, maybe even Bridie. Then I saw a light flick on in the Mullin cottage, all yellow, and I thought it would be a different winter, and I felt my cheeks warm, and, thinking I must be something like shy if I blushed knowing my own feelings, I dropped down on the bed and into the covers, liking the idea and liking me just a little bit more.